Disco Fries & Scenic Drives

Life in the Garden State

Edited by

S. Atzeni and Adam Wilson

Published by

Published by Read Furiously. First Edition - Trenton, NJ.

ISBN: 978-1-960869-22-7

Anthology | Short Stories | Poetry | Comics | Photography | New Jersey

For more information on *Life in the Garden State* or Read Furiously, please visit readfuriously.com. For inquiries, please contact info@readfuriously.com.

Read (v): The act of interpreting and understanding the written word.

Furiously (adv): To engage in an activity with passion and excitement.

Read Often. Read Well.
Read Furiously

Table of Contents

Order Up

Adam Wilson

Tetiana Horina

OPEN 24 HOURS
DINER
OPEN
STAFF ONLY!
DISCO FRIES & SCENIC DRIVES
Adam
HEY, WE NEED YOU OUT FRONT.
SURE THING. BE RIGHT THERE.
TIME TO GET BACK TO WORK.
STAFF ONLY!!!
DISCO FRIES & SCENIC DRIVES
SHALL WE?

It's time for round three, dear readers.
Disco Fries & Scenic Drives.
Another collection of work that strikes at the heart of the Garden State.
*DING DONG!
Quintessential stories of the New Jersey experience.
Ta-da!
And what's more quintessentially New Jersey than these monstrosities?
ADAM
In some places you'll find variations like poutine, in others loaded potatoes, but here in Jersey, they're Disco Fries.

A staple of the 1970s disco scene, they were created at a diner, no different from this one, for the bridge and tunnel set coming home from a night dancing at the clubs in New York City.
Designed to be the perfect combination of salt, grease, and carbs, the goal was to sop up as much alcohol as possible to help hedge your bets against a morning hangover.
They started popping up on more and more menus and their popularity grew to the point where they've become pretty much synonymous with New Jersey diner culture.
ADAM

And I share this little culinary fun fact because it circles back beautifully to the title of our collection: Disco Fries & Scenic Drives.
ADAM
See, New Jersey is one of those interesting places. It's small, the fifth-smallest state in the country, but we cram a lot in here - actually, we cram pretty much everything in here.
SHOP
You can drive through New Jersey in just a couple hours. But in that time, you'll pass through almost the entirety of the United States.
You'll see cities and farmlands, the main streets and the shorelines. The beauty of the natural world and the harshness of the industrial scape.
We have every view you could ever want.

Every scene outside your window is a reflection of somewhere.
A microcosm of everything that is the United States. Not just the places, but the people too, the stories. It's all of us. It's a local sports legacy, a trip with friends. It's scandal at the mall and a massive winter snowstorm. Moments of quiet contemplation, and moments you just can't comprehend.
Still don't be fooled, you'll see yourself in these stories, but in the same way that one would never truly call Disco Fries poutine, these are stories that are undeniably New Jersey as well. Something so distinct, and yet so universal.
So strap in as we once again explore Life in the Garden State. The stories of us, stories of you, the stories of everyone.
ADAM
ADAM

And maybe grab a snack for the road.
Disco Fries & Scenic Drives
Disco Fries & Scenic Drives
The End

The Vigilantes in Aisle Three
Danielle Robertson

The advent calendars show up the day after Thanksgiving.

The boxes are dropped off by a truck during the morning shift on Black Friday. Marissa and I wait at the loading dock, bundled in our winter coats. Our hands are stuffed in our pockets, and our breath puffs out of us in white clouds that could give Brad's cigarettes a run for their money. We wait in silence as the delivery driver hops out of his seat and pulls open the door of the cargo bed. The door squeaks as it lifts, the loudest of sounds in the early morning air.

"You girls are here early," the driver says. He's chewing peppermint gum. I can smell it from six feet away. I wonder how long his shift has been. Is this the beginning of the day, or the end of it?

"Not enough coffee in the world," Marissa says. She's surprisingly cheerful this morning, or at least, her Resting Bitch Face is a little less threatening. Probably because she's only working for three hours and then she's off to meet up with that boy from Morristown. Plus, she has a hazelnut latte waiting for her in the break room.

The coffee I guzzled in my family's kitchen—swiped from the pot before Mom could get to it—is a distant memory.

"Well, you look fresh as daisies," the driver says.

"Why does a health and beauty store need to open early for Black Friday?" I ask Marissa.

We watch the delivery driver unload the boxes from the cargo bed onto our metal dollies.

"God, don't you know anything, Larry?" Marissa says. "There's a sick deal on Q-tips."

The delivery driver laughs, exhaling cold peppermint.

"You two are a riot," he says.

We stop talking because it's weird having an audience. Especially when it's a guy who might be old enough to be my dad. The driver loads the last of the boxes onto the dollies just as Brad steps outside, looking way too awake for the hour.

"Good morning," he says. "I'll initial that."

The driver hands him his tablet. Brad pulls out the nerdy little stylus he keeps in his shirt pocket and scrolls through the order summary before signing with a flourish.

"Alright, let's get this inside," Brad says.

"And get these girls inside," the driver says. "They're freezing!"

I breathe in the smell of the break room. It's a perfume of cold metal, and circulating heat turned high, and the smell of hazelnut coffee. A trace of cleaning products lingers, the fake lemon weaving its way across the floor.

"Isn't it late for advent calendars to just be getting in? December is only a few days away."

Marissa rolls her eyes. "Which means that these will need orange clearance stickers on them before we know it."

The cardboard advent calendars are printed with cheerful Christmas scenes, punctuated by boxed outlines that contain numbers one through twenty-four. A child (or chocoholic adult) can open a box each day leading up to Christmas Eve and be rewarded with a small square of chocolate. Or one could scramble to open all twenty-four boxes in one sitting and eat twenty-four waxy milk chocolates in rapid succession.

I take the stock out to aisle one. The calendars will take up the spots vacated only yesterday by leftover Halloween candy.

I yawn and dream of coffee. All I can think about is how Marissa's right: these will have clearance stickers on them in a few days.

#

There's something jarring—unnatural—about hearing a scream in the haircare aisle.

Marissa and I lock eyes across aisle one, where we've finished putting out advent calendars and have been tidying up the travel section.

The scream rings out again. It's shrill and panicked, and someone else shouts "Woah."

I reach into my apron pocket and grip my phone. My heart is pounding and my throat tightens. But there is no slam of bodies or gunshot noise; there is no stampede for the door.

We're halfway to haircare when Colin appears, red-faced and grinning.

"There's a hamster running along the shelves."

Marissa's caffeinated laughter bursts out of her like steam.

"A hamster?" She asks.

The flurry of voices has us moving towards the haircare aisle, and we hear the jingle of Brad's keys as he hustles from the back room towards the commotion.

"Everyone alright?" He asks, glancing at us before turning towards the customers. I can see the panic in his eyes, amplified by his glasses. I can tell he's taking stock of the scene: the cans of hairspray that have clattered to the floor from the middle shelf. A customer's basket turned on its side, spilling out toothpaste and pantyhose.

An old man is peering down a stretch of shelving. He's waving his finger and saying to Colin, "The little bugger went that way."

Two little boys crouch at the end of the aisle and peer down the line of shelves, practically humming with excitement.

One customer, a woman who is pale and trembling, clutches at Brad's arm.

"It ran across my foot!"

I turn away, feigning vigilance, casting my eyes to the floor. I'm about two seconds from laughing.

And then I lock eyes with it. The hamster. And the breath whooshes out of me in a gasp.

One of the boys shouts. The hamster is fuzzy and white, and its black eyes look like little liquid buttons. The poor thing is shaking, peering out from behind a bottle of anti-frizz serum. Out of the corner of my eye I see Colin move towards it, like he's set to barehand the hamster like a baseball, and the stillness is broken.

"Open the front door! Open the front door!" The old man shouts from his crouch.

"Don't open the door! The poor thing will get run over by a car on 287, or freeze to death," Marissa says. "A hamster popsicle!"

The hamster bolts, knocking three bottles of serum to the carpet below, and the lady screams again. The old man cackles, slapping his hands against his knees. The boys run in the direction of the hamster.

"Okay, okay," Brad says, still calm, but the undercurrent of stress crackles through his words like a live wire. "Colin," he grinds out. "Go over to Pet Paradise and bring an… associate over here."

"You're going to need to get the health department in

here," the woman says, an edge of hysteria in her voice.

For some reason I imagine the health department invading Barrow's like a SWAT Team, with people in protective gear and hazmat suits overrunning the place. Rolling caution tape across the entrance to aisle three. Bagging hamster poop from along the edge of a shelf. All of us fingerprinted, swiped at for fibrous hamster hairs, interrogated under the harsh fluorescents. Marissa laughing out of nervousness, Colin cracking an ill-timed joke. The thin line of sweat at Brad's hairline is the only indicator of him being shaken.

"I'm sure there's a logical explanation for this, ma'am," Brad says. "Larissa, can you please escort our customer to the far register to help her check out today?"

Pleased with the idea of an escort, the woman lets go of Brad's arm and looks me dead in the eye.

"I forgot my coupon at home," she says, like a challenge.

"I'm sure Larissa can accommodate you," Brad says.

Colin, red-faced, runs back into the store with an apathetic-looking pet shop employee. The guy looks like he just rolled out of bed and threw on a hoodie. His hands are stuffed in his pockets, and he does not look as frantic about the escaped hamster.

The customer shivers as she hands me her basket of toiletries.

"Did you have a nice Thanksgiving?" I ask, as cheerful as I can, my eyes darting between the task in front of me and the direction of the scuffle.

"Do you think it came through the vents?" the woman asks, peering up at the ceiling like a shower of hamsters is about to rain down on us.

"I can't believe it'll be December soon," I continue.

"What?" she asks, finally looking at me. "Am I going to get my coupon?"

#

"Wait, wait, let me get this straight," our coworker, Rob, says, through a mouthful of spinach pizza. "The hamster scurried over the lady's foot?"

Colin's laughter booms big and bright in the back room. "Dude, you should have heard the scream that came out of her."

"She was wearing ballet flats," I say. "No socks. Which made it even worse."

Marissa, whose shift ended fifteen minutes ago, is perched on the table near the time clock, bundled up in her winter coat.

"Serves her right for wearing ballet flats in November."

The hamster had gotten in through the back hallway that's shared between Barrow's and Pet Paradise. Surprisingly, this is not the first time this has happened, but there still isn't any protocol in the employee handbook about how to handle Hamster Skirmishes.

"You should have seen the poor thing," I tell Rob. My eyes get watery, thinking about the soft little face, peering up at us from a prison of shopping baskets and old aprons. The hamster's eyes were pleading with us—I just know it—like it wanted us to reconsider sending him back to Pet Paradise.

"He's probably telling the other hamsters about his daring escape," Rob says.

"He's probably bragging about how much shit he left

along the base of the shelf in aisle three," Colin groans. "Little pellets, like chocolate chips, that I had to vacuum up."

"Eww," Marissa whines.

"At least he stuck to the aisle with the fake camera," I whisper. "No video evidence."

"An experienced deuce-dropper," Colin shakes his head.

"Screw Big Brother," Rob says. "No video evidence."

Marissa's boots make one more clunk against the cabinet, and then she's up and winding her scarf around her neck.

"I'm late for an appointment," she says, her mouth quirking.

"Thanks for coming in so early, Marissa." Brad appears in his office door, clutching his paper coffee cup so hard that the sides curve inwards.

"As long as everyone got their Q-Tips, I'll say it was all in a hard day's work."

Brad smiles and shuts his office door. Marissa smiles at the closed door and says, "But do *not* put me on the schedule for next Black Friday."

Colin shakes his head. "The advent calendars are late this year."

"They'll have stickers on them by next week," Rob says.

"That's what Marissa and I were saying this morning!"

"I gotta get one," Colin says. "They're in aisle one, right?"

"Seasonal section," I say. "Can't believe the hamster passed those by."

At the end of my lunch break, Colin and Rob are there to greet me in aisle one. Rob's hands are stuffed in his apron pockets, and he gives me a little smile.

"Larry," Colin says, his own smile megawatt. "We have an

idea…”

#

I made a joke around Halloween this year. Spurred on by a customer in a medieval costume and the need to make my coworkers laugh.

A joke about fake cameras in the aisles of Barrow's. The perfect opportunity for Robin Hood and his Band of Merry Men to swoop in, steal health and beauty products from the rich and distribute them to the poor.

And now Rob and I are standing in the loading dock with our hands in our apron pockets.

The tires make a smooth noise, like a zipper unzipping, as Colin's red pickup truck glides around the corner of the building. The truck idles for a moment and the brake lights come on. He maneuvers the bed of the truck back into the loading dock, just like we planned in our group text last night.

"We don't have much time," Rob says, hoisting a box up and into the bed. "I told Brad we were taking out the trash from the last pallet shipment."

"If only we were the employees who took smoke breaks," I say. "They act like they're all entitled to ten minutes. My lungs are healthy and I get nothing."

There were just so many advent calendars in aisle one.

Too many to sell before the need for them passed.

Who wants to start an advent calendar on the fifth day of December?

I pick up a box, too. Colin springs out of the driver's seat and stretches, grabbing the box out of my hands. The morning is cold, and when he exhales his breath makes giant clouds in the air.

"Let's hustle," he says.

"Larry, take this one," Rob says. We all fumble for a moment, because Coach Colin didn't exactly plot out our play-by-play on a whiteboard. But soon we get into a rhythm, pulling boxes out of a pallet and loading them into the truck bed.

"There are fifteen boxes here," Rob says. "Are we literally taking fifteen boxes of advent calendars?"

"If I wanted less than all of them I would've taken my dad's two-door," Colin says. "Do you think Robin Hood would half-ass this?"

The door of the loading dock is open, and the noise of the storage room sounds far away.

It was so easy.

Wheeling the boxes of advent calendars on our metal cart, back down aisle one, all the way to the back door. The door to the hallway that's shared with Pet Paradise.

The door that leads—in a slightly labyrinthian way—to the loading dock.

It was so easy, in an aisle outfitted with a fake security camera.

"Larry, if you're not going to help, at least go be on the lookout."

So I wander back towards the storage room door and try to calm down, and pretend that all of my jokes were not just thinly-veiled attempts to tamp down the fact that I'm freaking out.

We're stealing company property.

And it was sort of my idea.

Okay, so it was really Colin and Rob's idea. But I'm the one who made a joke about the fake cameras. I'm the one who made a throwaway joke eons ago about being The Robin Hoods of Barrow's, in an effort to make the team laugh.

I wheel a dolly with a squeaky wheel against the door, like the bedroom bureau blockades I always see in horror movies.

I try to pretend that I'm not an accessory to the heist of the century. I try to figure out how I'm going to walk back to the front of the store and act normal for four more hours.

And then: the storage room door is being pushed open. The wheels squeal before the dolly slides out of the way. My heart jumps into my throat because Brad's black tennis shoes appear through the doorway before he can force his shoulders and head through.

His glasses flash in the fluorescent light. "Larissa," he says. "Are you and Rob almost done? We could use at least one of you on backup."

I can't turn around to look back towards the dock. I tell myself that if I can't see it happening, it's like it never really happened. Maybe Brad's eyesight is too bad to make out the scrambling shapes of Rob and Colin—Colin, who's not even working today—and the glaring red blot of the pickup truck. Maybe...

"There was a dude who was looking for moving boxes," Rob says from behind me. "I gave him a couple, since we were recycling them, anyway."

"Rob, that's fine," Brad says. "But that's not really company policy. But it's fine."

"That's really nice to hear," I say. I don't know if I'm

talking to Brad, or Rob, or Colin's truck, undoubtedly speeding out of the parking lot in a blur of red.

#

From my post at the front of the store, I daydream of zipping down the parkway in Colin's truck, the stock of stolen advent calendars rattling around in the bed like a box of puzzle pieces.

"Larissa," Brad's voice splashes over me like a bucket of cold water. "Everything alright over there?"

I wonder if I somehow got chocolate under my fingernails from an errant melted advent calendar chocolate. Rob had so badly wanted to open one of the calendars, had wanted to "enjoy the spoils of our labor," but I told him that Robin Hood didn't go around eating the food meant for the peasants when he was redistributing the wealth, so neither would we. All of the calendars would go to the food pantry a few towns over, where families could pick one up to add to their grocery haul.

"Yes, everything's all good!" I cringe at the enthusiasm in my voice, but Brad smiles and pushes his glasses back up on the bridge of his nose.

"That's great to hear," he says. "Would you mind following me over to the office for a second?"

Rob glances at me from the supplies closet, his eyes big as saucers.

My heart plummets to my shoes.

#

"Close the door, Larissa."

Brad sits down in the leather computer chair at his desk. The chair makes a faint "poof" noise when he sits, the kind of noise that would normally set me giggling out of awkwardness, but my laughter has frozen in my throat.

I'm surprised I was even able to walk over here, with my heart getting all tangled up in my shoes.

"Take a seat."

I don't so much sit down as my legs give out from under me and, thankfully, there's a plastic folding chair below me to catch my fall.

"So," Brad continues. "It seems like you've been getting close with the other employees here at Barrow's."

He must know about the Robin Hood scheme.

He's going to make me squeal like that Pet Paradise hamster.

"They're a great bunch of people," I manage to say, my throat closing up around the words.

Brad nods at me, slowly. The overhead lights of the office reflect off the lenses of his glasses, making his eyes unreadable.

I don't want to lose my job.

"They are a great bunch of people," Brad says. He pauses and scratches his chin. I risk a glance at the monitors mounted to the wall, showing bird's-eye views of the aisles.

The aisle with real cameras, at least.

I don't want to go to jail for stealing.

"They're a great bunch of people," Brad repeats, and clears his throat. "Which is why I'd like you to help lead them."

"What?" My heart, discarded on the floor, flops to life like a fish determined to survive.

Brad leans forward, and I can finally see his eyes. They're crinkling at the corners.

"I'd like to appoint you, Larissa, to the position of Point of Sale."

"Oh, wow." I say. The position of a Point of Sale Associate - I'd learned from the employee handbook - is above a normal employee but still below a managerial position.

"You'd become responsible for some inventory level monitoring," Brad ticks off points on his fingers. "Scanning in orders. You'd have a key to handle transactions that require them at the register, like returns."

"Oh, wow," I say again. My heart isn't just flopping now, it's flip-flopping, doing somersaults and tumbles.

Brad smiles. "There will, of course, be an increase in your hourly rate, reflected in your next paycheck."

"That's great," I say, again, my mouth unable to form any other phrase.

"You're a hard worker, Larissa," Brad says. "We've all noticed how much you really care about the customers. How much you care about the store."

I feel a piece of my heart creak and crack off, like a chunk of ice in an ice floe. A frozen hamster skittering across a highway.

#

"Did you hear the news?"

Rob fumbles through his big sweatshirt pockets and pulls

out his phone, thrusting the screen at me.

GOOD SAMARITAN SPREADS SWEET HOLIDAY CHEER

My fingers tingle as I scroll farther down on the screen. And the images accompanying the post make my heart sing.

A group of food pantry volunteers, bundled up in jackets and earmuffs, hold stacks of cardboard advent calendars in their arms.

A closeup of a child's chubby fingers, prying open the Day 1 square on the calendar.

We have been Blessed! The post reads. *Imagine our volunteers' Surprise when they arrived at the pantry in the morning and found a stack of boxes waiting by the door. A truly sweet Gift from a Good Samaritan. Inside each cardboard box were a Treasure Trove of advent calendars ready to celebrate the Advent season. Wintery scenes, scenes of swirling snow and crackling fireplaces… it truly Warmed our hearts! Our volunteers passed out the calendars to families as they left the pantry over the last few days, and they were definitely a Hit! Let's remember the Reason for the Season!*

"That's…" I start.

"Isn't it awesome?" Rob's smile pops the dimple in his cheek, and I feel myself softening.

"The capitalization is inspired," I say. "Blessed, Surprise? Warmed? Hit?"

"Larry, you're a nerd," he says.

The metal of my POS key digs into my palm, hot like a crucifix against a vampire's skin.

"It should say Good Samaritans, plural," I say. "It was a group effort."

#

On my way out to the parking lot, my heart thrumming in my chest from the adrenaline of the successful heist and the unexpected surprise of a promotion, I hear my name being called from the direction of the pizza place.

"Hey, I heard the news!" Marissa shouts. She's shoving the remains of her pizza crust into her mouth, balling up her napkin and paper plate for the garbage bin.

I meet Marissa halfway between the pizza place and Barrow's, framed by the neon glow of fish tanks in the Pet Paradise window. She's sporting raised eyebrows and a new hickey on her neck.

"Yup," I say. "Kind of a whirlwind day."

"Don't downplay it!" she bumps me with her shoulder.

"I have a shiny register key and everything."

"Point of Sale," Marissa whistles. "Don't forget us little people on your climb to the top."

"I'd like to thank The Academy," I say in my snootiest voice.

Marissa laughs. "Seriously. Don't turn on us now."

I feel my smile drop. "You can't be serious."

She shrugs. "Just saying, there's usually a reason the Point of Sale's nickname is POS."

My laugh is hollow.

"Well, I should get inside," she says. "The stocking stuffers won't unpack themselves. I can't believe I missed this morning! Was it epic?"

"It was insane," I say. "Like something out of a James Bond movie or something."

Marissa shakes her head. "I need to be here for the next one."

"The next one?" I ask. But Marissa is already walking past me, wiggling her fingers in a goodbye wave.

In the front seat of my car, I let out a breath. I turn the heater on and let the warmth soak into my fingers. The heat shushes at my face, warm and quiet, like a mom trying to calm down her toddler in the candy aisle. My shoulders, tense all day from adrenaline, finally slump.

She couldn't have meant it, right? *There's usually a reason the Point of Sale's nickname is POS.*

Piece of Shit.

No. Just a joke. A joke between friends. The kinds of friends that make loud, crude remarks and have everyone at the diner staring at them. The kinds of friends that have parking lot photo shoots and celebrate victories with candy and French fries. The kinds of friends that group text in a language no one else can understand, full of inside jokes about Merry Men.

And then my heartbeat kicks up in a gallop.

Did she say "The next one?"

Steal Heart

Elaina Battista-Parsons

Everything in life is somewhere else, and you get there in a car.
~E. B. White

How it's going:

Briar Cliff, NJ was quiet and dead. I parked my Honda Civic under a scraggly, empress of an oak, far from civilization and walked toward a car more colorful than anything I'd read in books. A 1987 Camaro that wanted to be purple even though it was truly royal blue, sat yards away from where I stood - pushing into the blend of the sunset behind it. The hilly bank on which it was situated made me anxious. One wrong turn and the tires would bust all over the uneven terrain. When Rick was alive, he taught me about sports cars and their poor handling on ground not designed for tires. If it wasn't level and smooth, well, *Disaster*, he said. *Like sex after a bean burrito.* The message was drawn onto the glass on the passenger side, FOR SALE *$3500 FIRM*. Call 555-7620. Rick's voice echoed in my head: *it's not stealing if you put the car back where you found it. NJ is the land of cars for sale on grassy pull-over spots. Piss and gasoline.*

I felt for a key under the driver's side floor mat. Nothing. Under both front seats my fingers rummaged through leaves and *goddess* knew what else - no luck. I flipped down both visors to missing mirrors and a single papier-mâché poppy. I remembered Rick once looking inside the cassette deck of a van, but ever so delicately, or the key would get lodged in, and then you'd be screwed, along with the owner. This hobby was exhilarating in its wrongness, but so right in its rush.

Using a pen from my backpack, I reached past the key

that I hoped was there and positioned my other index finger to hold the cassette slat open. It was a fragile operation. I watched the key drop to the middle of the gearshift area and land on *R*. A shiny and silver key, clearly a brand-new copy. I attached it to my orange rabbit foot keychain and twisted my find into the ignition. Camaro hummed quietly. The plush black steering wheel smelled like fake lemons. A thousand fake lemons. I rolled down the window and veered off gently over the grass, highly aware of the hill I was dealing with as I maneuvered the steering wheel. Missing the cracked curb by an inch, I managed my way down to the road.

The roads were empty that evening, and I recalled a spot Rick told me about called Lambert's Creek. My gut told me it was after the left on Meghan Road. Creek was a strong word, as Rick described it as more of a very large puddle with nothing but swamp grass, ass-stinking water, and the occasional mosquito. But still, he spoke of it fondly as if it were a place he'd recommend seeing, then promised he'd take me one day. I remember where we were when he said the words, "One day I'll show ya the oversized sulfur puddle where I can hear myself think." We were rounding the tricky corner of Briar Cliff and Baobab Lane, and I commented on the FRESH EGGS sign that had an apostrophe where no apostrophe should ever be. Then I said, "Sounds lovely," and he playfully smacked my knee, our tension so undefinable. Like, it wasn't sexual, but it wasn't *not* sexual.

Yards later, the tires squished into a swampy cove and I parked Camaro on the most level chunk of land I could find. The rosebush was not an indication of some magical and enchanted place. The space before me was as Rick had described it—an oversized puddle in the shape of New Jersey. I walked towards the mucky, sulphury mess. The squelching of my sneakers was ripe, and I was unsure whether I wanted to stay in this brown place. I didn't feel drawn or curious anymore. I felt disappointed. I found a patch of celery-green grass and sat cross-legged with a straight spine.

I missed him. I missed our rides, up and down our state's deserted farm roads. Two lonely hearts full of boredom and tumult. A tiny frog pounced in front of me, then into the brush. Dusk embraced me, as the sun attempted one more jab at the day. I swallowed hard and fought lonely tears until I bursted out and cried like an animal. I tried not to moan, but it was so strong of an urge, and no one was near, so I surrendered.

Rick's process was simple:

1. You find the car and make sure the owner's *actual* car isn't in the driveway. If it is, you skip that FOR SALE.

2. You find the key. If no key is found, no hotwiring allowed. (Rick made an exception once while he was angry over his bandmates' argument)

3. Ride is a maximum of 15 minutes.

4. If you break down, you run.

5. Don't crash.

6. "The reason I'm not afraid of getting caught is because people in this town have better things to do than to babysit the thing they're trying to unleash." Rick's philosophy. His justification. His story.

Maybe Rick was this creek. My cries bellowed through the

darkening sky, but still a gentle swoop of brush startled me. I assumed it was in the tree branches kissing the water. Or maybe it's Rick finding something new to drum: *thrum, thrum, bam, boom*. My friend and his rhythm.

A white swan landed in this puddle. A gorgeous, black-billed swan with a bright orange beak floated in the blurry water. She was either unaware of me, or totally aware of me and acting aloof. I didn't speak swan, but I loved her. I loved her unabashed beauty. I wiped my face and focused on her snow-whiteness. I struggled to remember the shape of Rick's face, and as I rattled my brain for it, I heard footsteps in the mud a few yards behind me. I shot upright and whipped my body around, scaring the swan. Swan took flight. An older man with a confederate flag on his T shirt and a shotgun in his hand towered in front of me. My skin crawled, my jaw clenched, and a final tear escaped.

"And who the hell are you, young lady?" he demanded; his voice poisoned with years of smoking. His arms readjusted and his grip on the gun loosened at the sight of me. It kind of pissed me off that he might have thought I was helpless and couldn't destroy him with a swift kick to the gut.

"Get the hell outta here. I own the land.. Ya hear me?" He stomped his boot in the fudgy mud.

My hands were on Camaro in record time. Old man didn't seem like the kind of person who wanted to call the cops. He clearly handled things himself. I started the car and let my tears finish their explosions, driving toward the home base of Camaro. Reading was safe. Reading was danger. My mind entered a storm:

Cars encase us. Books too. We become surrounded by a good kind of cage. Barely shielded from outside debris, barely visible to the outside world. Cars and books fold us in and protect us from rage, rush, and trash. Cars comprised of glass, leather, plush, plastic, while books—paper and thread. Pages crisp enough to sometimes slice our skin and puncture our insides mostly, with squabble and turmoil of characters. I never noticed until recently, how much cars and books have in common. The dichotomy of cage and freedom provide—how they tease adventure, risk, high speed—down highways lined in green or gray, and where unexpected visitors can inhibit our space without permission.

I jogged back to my car despite the staggering heat. Adrenaline pushed me to the driver's side door, but not before I vomited my dinner all over the street. I stopped at 7-Eleven and chugged a gallon of water and scarfed down a package of Skittles before heading home to my bed where I buried the swamp at the back of my brain.

The Ridge Diner in Park Ridge, NJ. Maybe I'm biased, because Park Ridge is my hometown, but The Ridge makes a great BLT, a chocolate egg cream I dream about, and, of course, awesome Disco Fries. It was my favorite place to spend time with friends in high school, and now I bring my own kids there. But don't take my word for it: James Gandolfini—Tony Soprano in *The Sopranos* and a Park Ridge native himself—had also called out The Ridge as his favorite diner.

~Danielle Robertson (*The Vigilantes in Aisle Three*)

Favorite Diner - Rainbow Diner, Brick

~Kathy Kremins (*Selected Poems*)

When I was a kid, there was still a diner in the Pine Barrens, named Ong's Hat Tavern after an altercation that is said to have taken place in the woods there. The love triangle, or wormhole, or gathering place of oddball dissidents somehow made the hot wings, sandwiches and fries tastier. The place burned down mysteriously in the 2010s.

~Matt Lydon (*Platinum Platypus*)

Favorite Diner

Life in the Garden State

I love the drives through and around Hopewell, NJ.

~Elaina Battista-Parsons (*Steal Hearts*)

My partner and I like to drive to Warwick in the summers to go to the drive-in. The reservoir you pass on the way there can be pretty breathtaking if you catch it as the sun's going down.

~A.J. Pellegrino (*Somewhere in Between*)

Driving to Seaside Park via coastal roads.

~Gaveth Pitterson (*New Jersey: The Garden State in Pictures*)

Some of my favorite early memories are drives up and down the shore with my parents, ranging from Point Pleasant to Long Branch. The monolithic jetties, the timeless old houses, streets that seemed to come from different eras and that endless ocean...it always brings a smile to my face. Roll down your window. Let the wind ruffle your hair. Breathe in the salt air. Feel your soul renewed. That's life at The Shore.

~Scott Napolitano (*How The Story Ends*)

Best Scenic Drives

Meditations of a Hiker
J. E. Krantz

The soulless howl of the interstate reigns over the forest. I walk on dead leaves through a path of mud and rusty shopping carts, cast down from the A&P long ago, and carried away by the DuPont-polluted river. Both are now extinct. This is my New Jersey -- not a feral sewer of crime, not a concrete wasteland, and certainly not a pristine natural wonder. Hardly a "garden." But the river trundles on, its assailants forgotten, and the leaves still whisper, their voices nearly drowned in the endless drone of vehicles. Though faint, there is still magic here.

I carry a backpack bought from the Walmart on 23, and in my hand is a mystical weapon: my walking stick, a smooth piece of evergreen, barkless and golden, polished by Nature herself, found in the exotic lands of the Adirondack north; now a welcome traveling companion and safeguard against man and beast. But not against machines. For that, I rely on my camouflage hoodie to conceal me as a band of roving ATVs pass by, exalting in the size of their mud spray. They cross the river and move out of sight. Soon I can no longer hear them. I continue my journey.

I ascend out of the river valley, beneath the ever-present shadow and roar of 287. These little bumps and hills we call "mountains." The range I'm currently traversing is called "Ramapo," but the area is better known by its more patriotic title: "Cannonball Trail."

The path is padded with soft dirt, and I am careful to avoid the scorched, acrid pillars of charcoal that were once Ash trees, sacrificed in a bid to destroy the invading Red Jumpers. These trees were deliberately fired and poisoned to stop the spread of the "Spotted Lantern Fly" - not the only bad thing we picked up from the East in the last five years. Surely not the last.

I climb on. My journey has purpose - and it is not the destination. Deeply, I ponder the meaning of it all: not as one who sits writing, or sits reading; not as you or I, but as an objective observer. Why? Why the carcasses of ash trees? Why the soiled river, why the shopping carts? Why the endless drone of cars? And why is it so quiet?

All around me, the forest is utterly still, beaten into silence by the proximity of Man. Another DuPont relic stands before me - the corner of a brick building with lofty windows at a height of twenty-five feet. The corner is all that remains, and so it appears to me like some ritual site, some pagan altar. At its base is a firepit, littered with beer cans and surrounded by a tangle of tire-tracks. Once, this might have been a glade, where fifty or sixty deer fled before a hungry mountain lion; or where a fox hunted vermin in the brush. Now those creatures are obscure. Few know that the lion still lives here.

But I do. Because these are my lands, and I walk them; I experience them. I see all that I may -- from the rural motherland of Sussex to the hidden jewels of Bergen, I scour the world for signs of Life.

I stoop. I pluck a leaf from the soil. It is muddied, but whole, and unstained. I wipe it clean with tender fingers. I set down my pack, and withdraw a book. The leaf - for its color, for the valor displayed in preserving its shape and vibrancy until my arrival -- finds a new home between the pages of my journal. May all courage be rewarded.

To neglect such things is to trespass.

The way forward leads me through a hedge of thick

bushes and over a rocky portion of the trail, washed out by rain. I climb a bit more. The endless moan of the highway rattles the trees ahead. I'm close.

I emerge on a footbridge, covered by a tunnel of green chain-link fencing. The arched roof gives one a queasy feeling, as the overcast sky beyond is featureless. Beneath my feet, powerful concrete protects me from a fall to incalculable loss - and below, the Highway.

We have ascended to the pinnacle of Cannonball Trail, where the winds of the interstate are never stilled, and the silence of night is continually shattered. A place of travel; a city of transient people; a moving, shifting, vying suburb on wheels. Each human travels mindlessly to their next place. Daily I take this road myself, to the edges of Hawthorne and Wyckoff, to work. But I wonder how many have seen it from up here...

I can see the drivers as I look down from my perch on the bridge. They seldom see me. The angle is bad, and there is sun glare behind me. Would they look, if they could? So few see this land as I do. Fewer all the time. So few show real awareness for the world around them. We are lost in the miasma of the great City, of Babylon, always promising more, always giving less. If you can make it in New York, you can make it...in any other urban setting with law enforcement, hot-dog carts, highrises, and pavement. But you cannot make it "anywhere." Even here, thirty minutes from the city, most of these people would not survive without Starbucks - or at least QuickChek.

Sorrow demands an answer. Are they any different than the trees and the trails? Shouldn't they be mourned like the cougar and the fox? Where is the dignity of Man? Where is the lost beauty of powerful hunters with bows and spears, of singing maidens, of farming wives in fields of golden grain? The earth is ours to preserve and to love - and so is our neighbor. What else have we forgotten?

My objective reached, I take the homeward trail. Not all is gloom - not all is lost. Flowers appear as I trudge downhill, and I take a moment to appreciate them. I missed them on the way up - spindly weeds with tiny petals, a purple so pale it's almost white, and a bright, yellow center. A single bee finds them and shares my joy. The sunset is gorgeous, though obscured by the long branches of aging trees.

The light fades, and I navigate the mud carefully. I'm out before dark. I must return home, and sleep, and be fit for my shift tomorrow. I must pay my tribute of noise on the interstate; until, one day, I take the great Highway in the sky. There, in lofty throng of woodland creatures, over fields and forests, I will revel in leaves that never fall.

May all courage be rewarded. To do less is to trespass.

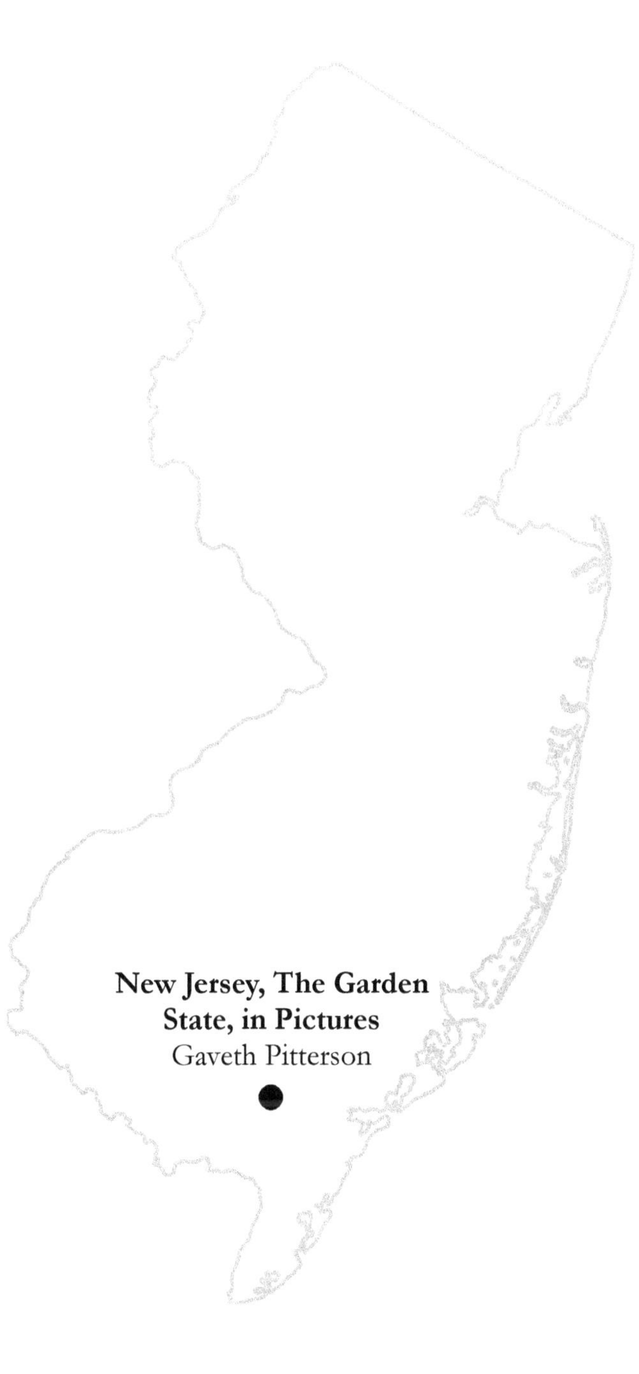

New Jersey, The Garden State, in Pictures
Gaveth Pitterson

Long summer walks in the woods under a canopy of trees. Enjoying nature's beauty including the sights, sounds and smells.

*Soft sand and gentle waves make this lake worth
visiting on a hot summer day.*

Lush green trees, birds chirping, fresh morning breeze as we make a pit stop during a leisurely ride in the park.

To be as free as this Hummingbird. Buzzing around the plants in my garden searching for nectar. Always a lovely sight.

New Jersey has many beautiful rivers and wondrous waterfalls. The sound of the water against the rocks and the mist carried by the slightest wind is so refreshing.

Springtime fun in the outdoors. The joy of picking tulips while enjoying all the vibrant colors as we welcome the new beginning.

Homegrown organic vegetables from our backyard; after all, this is the Garden State.

Fall in the Garden State is awe-inspiring - from the vibrant colors of the leaves to the cooler temperatures.

Postmarked Flagtown,
NJ 08821
Midge Guerrera

Sometimes the smallest action can bring the biggest visceral reaction. Having a bad day and needing some comfort food, I opened a can of crushed tomatoes to start a pot of pasta sauce. The scent of those tomatoes absolutely broke me and then bucked me up. My mind raced back years to growing up in Flagtown, New Jersey and Aunt Catherine. My savior and the strongest, most focused and smartest woman I ever knew. We often made sauce together with me learning more than how to slice and dice. All my young life when chaos raged at home and adult life when my world spun out of control, Aunt Cat was my sanctuary and teacher. I often found Postmaster Cat sorting mail or doing the books in the Flagtown Post Office.

Did you know that Flagtown was a small village in Hillsborough Township, Somerset County, New Jersey, the United States of America, North American Continent and the World? I did, because someone sent a letter to the Flagtown Post Office and that was the address they used. The World!

Around the Fourth of July and Flag Day, a lot of people from all over sent letters to the Post Office. Inside would be a postcard addressed back to the person and a note. The note would say, "please cancel the stamp close to June 14th or July 4th and mail the card back to me." Aunt Cat said these people were stamp collectors and a cancelled stamp from the only town in the USA called Flagtown was super important to them.

Flagtown was super important to me too. It is where I grew up in a red house, just up the dirt path from Grandma's house, over the corn field to Uncle Tony's, and down the grassy hill to the Post Office. Uncle Nick's house was across South Branch Road, and until I was ten, I couldn't cross it alone. I could go to the other houses and the Post Office whenever I wanted.

My Flagtown was Sunday and Thursday pasta with everyone crushed round Grandma's plastic covered kitchen table. Everyone – Aunt Cat, Grandma, Uncle Sal, Uncle Nick, Aunt Julie, Roseann, Uncle Tony, Randy, Bobby, Maryellen, daddy, mommy sometimes and my baby sister, Suska. We shared one mapeen to wipe the sauce off our fingers. Everyone laughed as that dishtowel got tossed from saucy face to saucy face.

Flagtown was Farley's Tavern where little girls could sit on the pool table playing with dolls while the big people socialized and political deals were made. It was DeScala's butcher shop, Clawson Machine Shop, Kane Bus Garage, Firehouse Company Three, wild strawberries, goats, sheep, fields and bicycles.

What was so cool was that at the Flagtown Post Office

people had to ask for their mail. You couldn't open the postal box door from the other side. There was no door. Just little pigeon boxes facing Aunt Cat. That meant that everyone had to talk to my Aunt Cat. Always smiling – even on crappy days - she knew everyone and everything.

The Flagtown Post office wasn't always the kingdom of the best aunt that a niece could have. In this rural village, there are as many versions of how Aunt Cat got to be postmaster, landlord, property developer, and my best pal as there are for how Flagtown got its name. Was it named after Mr. Flagg who bought up lots to develop small summer houses or because Flagtownians would stand by the railroad track and flag down the local trains?

Historians who research this stuff said the post office started in 1910 as a shelf in the Jersey Central Railroad Station. Then during World War I, a persnickety railroad agent was hired who wasn't interested in handling mail. For about five years, mail was sorted and distributed out of The Clawson Machine Company. Whisk in the 1920s and back to the railroad station it went.

Cheese Farley who spun a great story, and was my dad's best pal, over a beer at his bar told me, from 1936 to 1941 the post office had a corner in Buckshaw's general store - Jim Timberlake was the part-time postmaster. Then Catherine was made postmaster – getting us closer to the heart of this story- and they were freezing her out. The Buckshaws kept that place freezing - never had any heat - they kept a big sweater on a hook near the door that led to their house. When someone came into the store a bell would ring. Whichever Buckshaw was working would come in and put that sweater on.

Cheese said, "Catherine froze her ass off - they treated her like dog poop. We have the Flagtown Post Office so Catsy could have heat."

Do you want to know the real story? It is fitting that the real story of Aunt Cat's journey started with a letter. A letter that only the bravest of brave or desperate of desperate would have written. A letter that changed the life of an immigrant with a disability.

One year after mail started coming to Flagtown, Caterina Guerrera was born in Pontelandolfo, Italy to Rosaria Solla and Francesco Guerrera. As a bright, inquisitive and talkative toddler, Caterina raced over the hills of her village until she couldn't. Struck with polio, as many people around the world were, her right arm stopped growing, and she would drag her useless leg up the cobblestone streets.

The local priest strongly encouraged - *ahem*, tried to force - my grandmother to put my Aunt Cat in an institution. Instead, my grandmother got her family to Napoli and onto the SS Madonna. The cargo ship was built specifically to carry cargo and 1,650 emigrants in steerage to New York. (I'm thinking the emigrants were considered cargo too.)

Life experiences make us who we are. For little Caterina, the horrific crossing with a very ill mom and being quarantined at Ellis Island alone and not understanding a word of her captors gave her some true grit.

The family made their way to New Jersey and went through all the trials and tribulations that were thrust upon non-English-speaking immigrants by men and women who were one generation away from being non-English-speaking immigrants.

The entire family finally ended up owning a substance farm in Flagtown, New Jersey. A farm that fed us all. Goats, sheep, corn, vegetables and chickens.

WAIT A MINUTE! Back up! How did an immigrant with a disability get to be a United States Postmaster???

Pay attention: like I said, it began with a letter. A letter to Eleanor Roosevelt. This story is the story that shaped my family and definitely shaped me. One day, long after she retired from the Postal Service, while we were making her special sauce and meatballs, I got Aunt Cat to tell me everything.

"Mrs. Roosevelt's husband, the President of the United States, had polio. I had polio too, graduated high school, was accepted to college but we had no money. I could only find work in a sweatshop picking up the clothes the women at the machines dropped. It took them too long away from sewing to bend over and get the scraps. There had to be more for me."

"Twenty letters, I wrote. Twenty letters I burned in the back of the barn and the twenty-first I sent to Mrs. Eleanor Roosevelt. Democrats are for the people - not like Republicans who care only for the rich. Before Roosevelt there weren't any jobs. Then Roosevelt made jobs that helped the country. Sal was in Arizona with the Civilian Conservation Corps. I just knew that Eleanor Roosevelt would help me. I just knew it."

"One morning while I was working in the garden and babysitting Tony, a big black car came for me. This woman in a brown suit got out of the car and showed me some papers. She came from the state, and she said that she was going to take me to see a doctor who could maybe help me walk better. My father was working on the railroad, and my mother was with Julie's mother – I told Tony to tell Mama I'm going to see a doctor and I got in the car."

Being a chopping garlic skeptic, I asked, "Did the Roosevelts for sure send the social worker?"

"Of course – I sent the letter and the lady came. Eleanor Roosevelt was a great lady – not like these 'looking out for themselves movie star first ladies.' Mrs. Roosevelt cared about real people, not just rich people."

Having an a-ha moment, I asked, "Have you ever voted for a Republican?"

"Get the soap and wash your mouth. Do you want me to finish the story?"

"If I listen, do I still have to wash my mouth out?"

Aunt Cat tossed a meatball at me – which I caught and plopped in the sauce pot.

"If someone could help me walk without dragging my leg like a mail sack than I was

going. What I didn't know was that the doctor was in Newark – in those days you only

had Route 28 and it took 2 hours to get to Newark. The lady took me to Beth Israel Hospital –

Dr. Kessler himself saw me and asked me if I was strong. He said it would take 8 surgeries. He could make me walk better and my bad arm wouldn't just hang like a dead branch. But I had to be strong.

The doctor laughed when I told him that I milked the goats and cows, plowed the field following Mary the horse and dragged my leg the half mile to the train stop to go work in the sewing factory – strong – I was strong. Still strong enough now to roll these meatballs with one hand.

Old enough to sign the papers, the next thing I knew I

was in a huge room lined with beds. In those days you slept in a bed in a ward with 40 other beds. I wasn't even afraid. Dr. Kessler had this way about him – he cared – like the Roosevelts. After the first surgery Dr. Kessler asked the nurse why no one ever came to visit me. He asked me if I had any family. I told him my family lived in Flagtown – which to him was like living on the moon. I had left with the social worker and never went home. I thought she told my mother. I thought my little brother Tony told my mother. I thought the lady in the black car went back and told them that I was staying. What did I know? All I knew was that I was going to walk without dragging my leg.

Dr. Kessler asked me if I wanted to use the telephone and call them. I looked at him cross-eyed. You didn't have a phone in the depression unless you were rich. So, I wrote them a letter and told them where I was – the boys could read in English – as soon as they got the letter they came. All of them crammed around my bed. Mama was first crying and then furious that I wouldn't let them take me home. She wanted me to come right home – cast and all. She was so mad – all Tony said was some lady took me in a black car. They thought I got picked up as an enemy alien. Just a few years before during the war, Italian immigrants were picked up and tossed in internment camps. Italian prisoners of war were held just down the street at the Belle Mead Depot. They tried to deport my brother Nick, but somehow my father stopped them.

I felt bad, I got why she was scared and angry. After all the surgery, therapy and I could walk - she stopped being angry. I could walk almost normally, and I was strong. Strong enough to go back to the sewing factory."

Putting down the knife slicing tomatoes for salad, I looked at Aunt Cat and like a radio announcer said, *Boom! Magically, in the 1940s it was decided in Washington that Flagtown needed a dedicated full-time postmaster, and the job was offered to Catherine Guerrera. If she took the job, she would be paid on commission.*

"OK, know–it-all, stir the sauce," said Aunt Cat.

I stirred and Aunt Cat continued talking.

"My father told me that they were going to need someone to be the new full-time Flagtown Postmaster and I could get the job. Pop said – and he was right – the post office was a gift, and I could make it into something big. You didn't get a salary; you got a percentage of what you sold and how much came through. I was working in a clothing factory making $15 a week. Why should I take this and make only six or seven a week? Pop told me that it was an honor to be a postmaster in Italy.

I'm glad I listened to my father. Then, I got a pretty good income and now I get a good pension. Today, I read the papers and listened to my niece babble on. I miss that job. In the beginning in that corner of the grocery store, there wasn't much to do so I helped in the store. One night, I said to my father, since I do everything anyway, I might as well work for myself. I wrote a proposal, called and got permission from the government to build a free standing twenty- by-forty foot post office."

My father gave me a piece of ground. He and my brothers built me a small building, and we rented it to the government for the post office. The goat patch in front of our house became the first free standing Flagtown Post Office.

Then we told everybody we knew to only buy stamps

there and send their mail from there. Before I retired, I built that little place into a first-class post office. With my good arm I lifted the mail bags onto the truck – women didn't do that then."

I interrupted her story here because it set off flashes of memory in me. It was 1952 and clutching my three books for the month, I raced down the bookmobile steps – well I didn't really race, since my 4-year-old legs couldn't reach all the steps. The Somerset County librarian had to lift me down. In my head, I was racing down the steps to run directly into the Flagtown Post Office.

"See you next month," the library lady said as she climbed up into the van's high seat and pulled the Bookmobile out of the Post Office's dirt parking lot.

I waved and marched straight past the small ice cream freezer, metal rod shelf with bread, library reserve pick up box and penny candy rack. Without knocking, I opened the door marked "Post Office Employees Only." The Post Mistress didn't bat an eye. With her super powered left arm she hauled a canvas sack full of letters to the top of the narrow counter and dumped it. The metal brace holding up her right leg kept her steady and what she called her "baby arm" picked up a couple of envelopes.

Aunt Cat checked out my books and continued sorting the mail. I settled down with my books on a pile of canvas mail bags. She made sure the right person got the right letter. Just like people in a big city, Flagtown people had their own post office mailbox – it was free too. People liked coming to the post office, standing around sharing town gossip, chatting with Catherine and solving the world's problems. I liked coming the most.

"My brains were always working. After the war, Pop gave my brother Tony a piece of land to build a gas station – ESSO Oil. I figured people stop for gas, get mail – why not get a cup of coffee too. I decided to build an addition. I attached a two-story building to the post office that made the post office bigger. Now, I rented out upstairs apartments and had the Humble House Luncheonette with a jukebox and pinball machines. You worked for me, remember? Your first real job. I could never run the post office now, but I still get the rent check. Today it is computers for everything. I used to keep all the records in a book. I added pages of numbers in my head and never was short."

Wiping my hands on the sauce-red *mapeen*, I looked at Aunt Cat and asked, Did the Roosevelts really make that post office happen?

"When I came home from the hospital and needed a job, there wasn't one and then there was one. What do you think? Stir the sauce – enough conversation – I want to read the paper."

As the years passed, the Post Office and Aunt Cat's holdings got bigger and bigger. The modern Post Office has a lobby that doesn't feature candy and ice cream. Wooden mailboxes were long gone and brass ones with little doors arrived. No one has to ask for their mail and hold conversations with the postal employees. But no matter what, it is still the Flagtown Post Office. Something built by a disabled immigrant with grit, determination and the balls to write a letter to Eleanor Roosevelt.

Today, as I stirred my pot of sauce, a tear slid down my

face. Aunt Catherine's strength, diligence and foresight has always been there for me. The Flagtown Post Office, as it was, lives on in me and all those Flagtownians who came to gossip by the mailboxes.

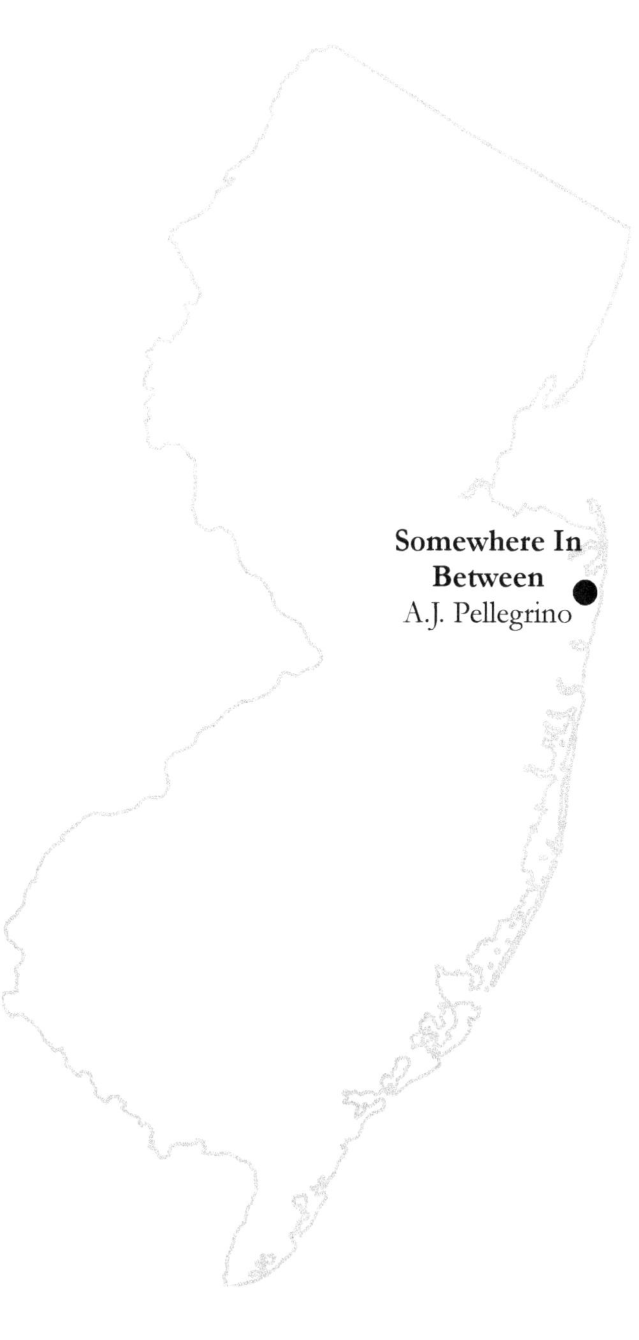
Somewhere In
Between
A.J. Pellegrino

The boardwalk is empty as Cam sits under the large gazebo. Its roof blocks out the rays of the magnificent full moon overhead. A quarter of a mile behind him, a large neon cross blazes atop the church that drew his mother to this beach in the first place. Cam's back is firmly, defiantly, placed to it. He has no quarrel with this particular church or the people that worship within it – he knows very little about their theology or the congregation to be honest. Its only real sin at that moment, in Cam's eyes anyway, is being a church.

"You can't hold onto that grudge forever." Cam refuses to look beside him to where Parker's voice sounded. Instead, he stares out ahead of him, past the dull bulbs in the ceiling into the darkness beyond. Far off in the distance, over the expanse of dunes dotted with long tendrils of grass that sway in the summer breeze, Cam can hear the crashing of the waves. "Hello, earth to Cam," Parker tries again. And again, Cam ignores him. So, Parker tries a different approach. "Mom was only doing what she thought was best."

It's strange to hear such grown-up sentiments spoken in such a young voice – prepubescent, still with a higher pitched quality to it that Cam's own voice had long ago grown out of. Cam's lips purse. It's just his own thoughts being regurgitated to him, he knows this. He and his therapist have spent so many sessions focused solely on this. And yet…

Cam turns his head ever so slightly, just enough to let his eye catch a glimpse of the figure sitting next to him before he snaps his head forward again. Parker never shows up in a haze of smoke or glowing aura. No, his brother always appears to him the same way – as solid and present as the day that riptide forced him under the water and stole the air from his lungs.

Cam knows Parker is looking at him expectantly. He always is whenever Cam finds himself near the sea. A trauma response, his therapist calls it. He and his mother both suffer from severe PTSD, though only he is taking the necessary steps to manage his condition. His mother does what she always does — shrouds herself guilt and piety and expects to heal.

"Why do you keep taking these trips if you hate them so much?" Parker voices the question Cam keeps asking himself. The question his therapist keeps asking. The question literally anyone would ask if they knew his situation.

"Because she needs me," Cam answers against his better judgement. He knows he's not supposed to talk to these manifestations of his own guilt. "She'd go regardless and then she'd call me crying until I came down here anyway. It's just easier this way."

"Easier for who?" Cam reverts back to silence in that question's wake. The long answer is that it saves time and emotional taxation for Cam to just go along with his mother's yearly pilgrimages to the waters that took her youngest son. It's just as unhealthy as the short answer — that it's simply easier to give his mother what she wants. And what she wants is to punish him. "You don't want to see me, do you?" Parker's sad tone tugs at Cam's heart. He must remind himself that his brother is dead. Whether the figure beside him is the symptom of a psychotic break or a ghost, Cam's always liked to believe the latter, it certainly isn't Parker. Especially since Cam doesn't always hate seeing him. Not really. And yet…

"Of course, I want to see you," Cam sighs. "I just – you shouldn't – it's not good for me."

Their mother used to say these episodes were Parker's spirit visiting him. She can barely contain her bitterness at the thought that her dead son refuses to grace her – his loving, devout mother – in such a way. Even now Cam knows he can't tell her that Parker's silhouette has haunted his every move since they arrived at this little strip of holy land on the Jersey Shore.

Tomorrow she'll spend the morning crying in one of the pews nestled in the church that sits closer to the heart of the town and Cam will sit on the sand with his brother's ghost sitting beside him. Then they'll meet up for lunch on the Asbury boardwalk like nothing was out of the ordinary. To anyone else they're simply a mother and son taking one last vacation after his graduation from college before he tries to get as far away from her as possible. Preferably somewhere land locked that's a bit more secular in its community, or at least more religiously diverse. But then…

If this is the last time he'll be near the ocean, Cam can't help the nagging want to turn his head. He doesn't want to fight the way his eyes drift back to his side pulling his head right along with them.

"See?" His brother beams through blue lips, water dripping from their center. The bloating of his face makes the round cheeks at the corners of his mouth even more pronounced and milky white eyes. "That wasn't so hard, was it?"

Parker has always been harder to look at in the dark, a stark reminder of what he looked like when they finally found his body. Cam realizes that he should have waited. Tomorrow in the sun, he'll have a lifelike illusion of his brother back.

Tonight, all he has is a corpse.

Cam closes his eyes almost immediately. Everything comes rushing back to him. It knocks the air from his chest as he doubles over trying to breath. The crashing of the waves is suddenly too close, too loud, all encompassing. He can practically smell the foul, gut wrenching aroma of formaldehyde mixed with the salt on the air. And that's when he feels a small hand on his back.

"I'm sorry," Parker says mournfully. It sounds distorted to Cam's ears, like he's the one who's been forced under water. All he can focus on is the immeasurable cold seeping through the fibers of his shirt from Parker's fingers. "I didn't mean to upset you. I never do. You know I can't control it."

Cam takes one shuddering breath, then another, and another before he wrestles back the bile in his throat.

"I know," he manages to choke out. "I know. It's okay. It's not your fault."

It's not your fault. The words Cam's heard a million times before.

"It's not your fault," his pastor told him at twelve. "Parker is with God now. Let that bring some comfort to you. He's gone home to the one who needs him most."

"It's not your fault," every one of his boyfriends has told him when he wakes up gasping for breath. "You were just kids. You can't blame yourself."

"It's not your fault," his therapist tries relentlessly to convince him. "Your mother was the one responsible for watching you both. You never should have been in that water to begin with."

"But I was the one she put in charge," he fights back over

and over and over again. "I should have been watching him."

It's his mother's words oozing out of his mouth. It's his mother's burning resentment that's been given the care it needs to fester and blister and scab over again and again. She's buried her rage deep inside his chest and tended to it, reverently, for all these years as she's coaxed Cam to repent for his sin.

"It's not your fault," Cam repeats. "You did the best you could." The words he's heard a million times before, except from the one person he's always needed to hear them from. He sits up, eyes still closed, and takes a deep breath. "I'm sorry, buddy." Cam forces out a chuckle as he wipes furiously at the tears on his cheeks. He won't look at Parker again – he can't – not until tomorrow. "I'm good now. I know you don't do it on purpose."

"It's okay," Parker assures him. "It's not your fault."

The infected manifestation of all that guilt buried deep inside Cam's chest throbs uncomfortably.

The pair sit in silence as morning approaches while the luminescent cross burns behind them and the ocean's tide slowly creeps away from the shoreline. The warm breeze of the summer night blows around them and Cam tenses as if that horrid smell is going to permeate his senses again. It does. There's no escaping it, but it's duller now – more manageable against the welcomed growing stink of low tide.

Cam's always wondered about Parkers shifting appearance. It's a thought he's never voiced to anyone, not even his therapist. He's not supposed to be indulging these moments, after all. But he can't help that it nags at him, even now. Especially now.

If Cam can manage to stay by his brother's side until the sun comes up, will he be freed from the grizzly appearance that haunts him? Will he get to witness the change from bloated nightmare to preserved memory? And if this is going to be their last few days together, well…

"Do you remember that game we used to play?" Cam's voice cracks as he glances towards his brother's spectral form again.

"I spy?" Parker sounds gleeful again. It was their favorite game to play from the back seat of the minivan on their way down to the beach every year. "Can we play I spy?"

"Yeah," Cam agrees. The emotional wound that their mother's spent so much time lovingly tending to pulses as Cam's stomach does a somersault. "Let's play. You go first."

"I spy," Parker pauses to consider his surroundings. Cam's eyes remain locked on the brightening sky. "Something that is…" Parker turns to kneel on the bench and stare back at the streets lined with cars that lead towards the city of tents that neighbor the church. Cam closes his eyes again as the clammy, icy cold of Parker's arm brushes against his own. "Something," Parker echoes as he searches around them for the perfect mark. Cam expects the bile to rise up his throat again, but it never does. "White!"

"White?" Cam questions, eyeing the numerous white objects around them. Parker never liked to go easy on him. Cam isn't sure if this is a confirmation that the little boy next to him is a hallucination or not. And right in that moment, he can't bring himself to care either way. "You sure?"

"I'm sure," Parker affirms.

"Alright," Cam doesn't fight the corner of his mouth that

tugs up ever so slightly. He twists in his spot on the bench to look around – trying his best to avoid looking down at his brother. He can't do it. Not yet. "White. White. Something white." Parker fidgets beside Cam before he starts to hum the countdown tune from *Jeopardy*. It's another moment where Cam wonders if this is just a long-buried memory come back to haunt him, or his brother made real before his eyes. "Is it the bench back there?" Cam points to indicate the correct one.

"Nope," Parker reveals, gleefully. "Two more."

The bright hues of the morning sky bleed through the inky blues to create a brilliant lavender color. Cam still doesn't risk a glance down at his brother.

"Is it the trimming on that house?" Cam guessed.

"Are you even trying?" Parker scolds him. "Only one more."

"White, white, white," Cam mutters as he turns fully in his seat now. "Something white. Something white."

"Do you give up?"

"No, I don't give up." Cam frowns as he looks back towards the ocean. Now that the sun is beginning to make its appearance, he can see more of his surroundings. "Is it that sign over there?"

"Not even close," Parker jeers. "Do you wanna know?"

"Of course, I want to know," Cam rolls his eyes. "What was it?"

"The big cross," Parker points behind them. "Back there. I can't believe you didn't guess it. You were staring right at it before."

Cam turns again to stare at the large symbol of loneliness. He can barely see how bright it is now when only an hour or so ago it shone like a beacon in the dark. It has to be safe to look upon his brother's face now. Surely the world is bright enough to chance a glance down at the very least. And if not now, when?

Cam looks down at his brother. Where once sat a ghoulish mockery of his memory now sits his little brother. Parker's bright eyes squint up at Cam as he smiles brightly. His skin in healthy and glowing, his hair as thick and windswept as Cam remembers.

"What to play again?" Cam asks.

"Fine but it's still my turn," Parker sticks out his tongue.

"Yeah, yeah, whatever you say," Cam nudges his shoulder. Warmth is all he feels now.

Maybe he can find somewhere to live that's close to the water. Maybe Cam can learn to visit his brother on his own terms.

All-Jersey Meal
Patrick Lombardi

Marcy packs her apron like a snowball and rolls it onto the dining counter. Her gaze is fixed on the swollen balloon of sunlight lasering through the front windows. The silhouettes of an elderly couple dissipate into the light as they exit Magissa Diner, a fresh gust of diesel wafting through the open doorway.

Not sunlight. High beams.

"Marcy, table seven needs another wipe," Mom's disembodied voice calls. "Looks like a bobcat ate there."

Marcy doesn't budge, forearms resting on the chrome trim wrapped around the Formica countertop like a chinstrap.

"Earth to Marcy," Mom calls again. "Put that apron back on."

By the time Marcy's eyes readjust to the waxy diner glow, Mom's already focused her attention elsewhere: to Dennis, the only guest at Magissa right now, seated at one of the dozen weathered booths while patiently waiting for his breakfast sampler for dinner. Marcy watches him say something with a smirk, and Mom tilts her head back to laugh, sliding a hand onto his shoulder to keep herself steady. Maybe this was an innocent, friendly gesture, but Mom pulls her hand away too quickly when she catches Marcy gawking. Then she sulks into the kitchen holding a mug stuffed with unused silverware.

Marcy feels her ears get hot as a tingling rises through her neck, like thousands of jabs from a needle against her skin. Her legs start pumping even before she decides she's ready to move, following her mom to the dishwasher in the kitchen.

"So that's why Dennis comes to this dump every day?" Marcy starts, no preamble.

Mom pretends to look confused. Or maybe she really is. "Don't talk about our restaurant like that," she replies. Her eyes are red around the black discs of her corneas. Wrinkles trail like tiny riverbeds across her forehead. Mom purses her lips and the lines dart inward like a barrage of arrows. "Your grandmother—"

"I know, I know," Marcy cuts in. "I don't need to hear the story again. Yia-Yia opened this place as a poor, single-parent immigrant. I'm proud of her. Really."

"Then show some respect," Mom says quickly. "If not to me, then to Yia-Yia." Before Marcy can respond, her mother looks down at her daughter's waist and asks, "Where's your apron? You can't leave yet."

"I'm meeting Sarah, Liz, and Becca down at the *bogs*."

"The bogs?"

"Cranberry bogs." Neither speaks for a beat, so Marcy jeers, "What's wrong? Ya think the *bog witches* are gonna get us? Carve us up for rituals? Feed our entrails to the Jersey Devil?"

"Stop that!" Mom waves her hand. "You're not going anywhere. You can't leave in the middle of dinner rush."

"*Dinner rush?*" Marcy questions. "You mean the *one* guy in this place? Your new *boyfriend?*"

Mom lulls her head as she tosses a fork into a bucket filled with God-only-knows-what kind of cleaning solvent. Then she squares up to her daughter. Jaw locked, her words slide through in a staccato rhythm. "Dennis and I are *not* in a relationship."

"Oh, so then just hooking up?" Marcy says, then squints.

Mom's jaw clenches tighter as she grinds the peaks of her teeth into place. A boxer bracing at the bell. "Don't you *dare* speak to me that way again. You're all I've got, and *I'm* all *you* have, too. Remember that. You think your little… *coven* of friends really cares about you? Would actually put their necks on the line for a friend?"

"You have no i—"

"No! *You* have no idea. I grew up in the pinelands, too. I know these people. They don't change." She blinks away the dampness in her eyes, then continues. "You want to hang out, drink, get high, forget about your problems—fine. Whatever.

In the last year, you've lost a sister and a father, so I don't blame you."

"That's not what we do."

Mom's face has fallen like a watercolor painting, blotched and bruised with sadness. Yet, her words stay sharp. "Don't B-S me, Marcy. Sarah's mom called three weeks ago. You think I don't know that she and Rebecca were picked up by Park Police? They had a bunch of... *herbs* on them. And mutilated frogs. Bugs and tiny *bones* in mason jars."

Marcy rolls her eyes.

"Thank God you weren't with them that day. I don't know what in the hell you're doing, but this is... entering a dark territory, Marcy." Mom clutches the crucifix around her neck.

How did Mom grab this interaction by the reins and completely divert its course so quickly? All Marcy can do is stare back at her mother.

"I was a stupid teenager too once," her mom continues, dropping both hands at her sides.

"Is that what you think of me?" Marcy chimes in.

Mom sees right through the feigned sadness. "All teenagers are stupid," she says, sliding past Marcy. "Adults are stupid, too."

"So we're *all* doomed."

Mom mutters over her shoulder, "We've always been doomed."

"I might as well leave then, right?" Marcy calls out as her mother increases the distance between them. "Before the whole world ends and I never see my friends again."

Her mother pauses, turns, and puts a hand up for a moment, pumping it back and forth with the rhythm of her words. "You can leave when the restaurant closes. That isn't changing. Don't ask me again."

Marcy watches her mother disappear through the kitchen

door. What Mom means, what she *really* means, is that Marcy will never leave the Pine Barrens, because this restaurant is going to stay open, conditions will never improve, and Marcy will be forced to wait tables here until everyone she loves has moved on. Marcy, the granddaughter of immigrants, would be a heathen to think that she could break free from the fate of this lineage. To even daydream about a life beyond these walls, beyond these woods. One in which she isn't charged with familial responsibilities.

Yia-Yia risked her life migrating five thousand miles to the *Land of Prosperity*. To envision a new kind of life would be to turn her nose up to everything her grandmother sacrificed.

Mom doesn't use those words exactly. It's written in the bags under her eyes, in the way she races out the door every morning before dawn, in the way she stands like clothes strung up on a hanger. *This is the* only *way*, her actions say.

But as Marcy steps back out into the dining room, she's sure Magissa *can't* be her destiny. The fossilized floral valances adorning olive-tinted windows, the smog of flaxen subway tiles like a prison hallway, the burgundy pleather booths and stools bolted to cracked concrete floors—this isn't the kind of diner New Jersey is known for. Marcy's seen abandoned buildings in better shape.

The bell above the entrance jingles, catching her attention, and a man steps in. He's dressed too nice to be here—Marcy initially thinks he might be lost. The sleeves of his baby-blue Oxford button-down are folded on mirrored angles halfway up the forearms, shirt tucked into a pair of twill chinos. With his gelled-back hair and scruffy, chiseled jaw, he looks like he's auditioning for an X-rated parody of *The Wolf of Wall Street*.

The man doesn't smile, doesn't greet Marcy. Just gives her a quick "One" while typing furiously on his Samsung.

Marcy waves a menu at him. "Right this way," she says and

guides him to the booth next to Dennis. The man halts, finally looking up from his phone.

"Here?" he questions, pointing at the table. "Entire empty restaurant and you seat me next to the *only* dude here." He gestures toward the tables on the opposite side of the entrance. "What about a booth over there?"

"That section's closed," Marcy replies, but he's already halfway there.

When he gets back near the entrance, he stops. "*Closed? What*—you can't walk the extra thirteen steps?"

"It's…" Marcy resets, perks up, decides she's going to give this guy what he wants. "Give me a sec. Let me clean a table off for you."

"The one at the end," Grumpy mumbles.

She pulls a damp rag from a bucket under the register and uses it to mimic a wipe-down of the table and cushions. As she lifts and fluffs a seat, she discreetly slides her hand underneath in a swift wave, like a magician motioning over a deck of cards. When she's done, she heads back up front. "All set," she says, and leads him back to the booth.

"Any specials tonight?" he asks as he scoots in.

"At a diner?" Marcy retorts, laying the menu, thicker than the Sunday paper, on the table.

He shrugs without looking up from his phone.

"Like a special pork roll or something?" she smirks, but then wipes her face clean.

The man curls his upper lip and wriggles his nose, disgusted. He finally locks his phone and looks up at her. "That sounds good to you?" Marcy opens her mouth to respond, but he puts up a finger. She wants to bite it off. "That's what you people are known for, right?" he continues. "That's, like, the only New Jersey staple." He grins for the first time, and despite his perfectly straight alabaster teeth, Marcy can't help but cringe.

"And maybe disco fries," she adds, more like a question.

"What's that?"

"Crinkle-cut fries covered in homemade gravy."

The grin fades. "*Mmm*," he mocks. "Thanksgiving for woods people."

Marcy grits her teeth. "Bet."

The man sighs and Marcy slouches. She doesn't want to be here any more than this guy does, apparently. She should ask why he even chose this place. Lucille's and Martucci's aren't too far. Vincentown is relatively close. Even Marcy and her friends go out of their way to Lacey Diner or Sand Castle Diner for "brinner" and dessert. All are legendary diners, unlike this one.

The man shrugs as he peruses the first couple pages of the menu. He lifts a hand to his forehead in a defeated salute. "Yeah, I guess give me the pork roll, egg, and cheese on a Kaiser with a side of disco fries."

"You sure?" Marcy asks reactively.

The man rocks his head side to side before readjusting to a nod. "Might as well, while I'm in town. I'll try an *all-Jersey* meal."

Marcy cringes. Out-of-staters saying "Jersey" hits differently. She hates it. But if that's what he wants, that's what he'll get.

"Salt, pepper, ketchup?" Marcy asks.

"On the sandwich?"

She nods.

Another sigh of defeat. "No ketchup."

The man goes back to his phone while Marcy slides the menu off the table. "And to drink?"

"Coffee. Black." Then he shoos her away like a fly.

After posting the ticket in the kitchen, Marcy dips out to the counter to pour the coffee. She pauses for a moment, staring into the mug. An inkwell in her hand. She drops in a teaspoon, watching the ripples ebb and flow like bog water in the wind. She stirs it, three complete revolutions, and whispers so low even she can't make out the words.

"Why don't you brew a new pot?" Mom mutters over Marcy's shoulder, startling her daughter. "That was brewed hours ago."

She's embarrassed, so lost in her thoughts that she didn't catch the aroma of Dennis's breakfast sampler lined up Mom's arms on graying plates. Two buttermilk pancakes like Frisbees on one, scrambled eggs and rye toast on another. Oily hash browns and thick-cut bacon each get their own.

Marcy heads to Grumpy's booth without a word. She plops the mug down and gestures to the end of the table. "Sugar and stuff are in the tray."

He doesn't say thank you as he puts his phone face down and snatches a handful of artificial sweeteners. With his elbow, he nudges a fork and a knife to the edge of the table. "These are filthy," he tells Marcy. "I need new silverware. *Spotless* this time."

Marcy inspects the utensils on her way to the dishwasher. A few watermarks, but nothing that would classify them as *filthy*. As soon as she gets to the back, she hears some rumblings in the front of house. A low voice that she thinks is Grumpy, so she delays her return to the dining room. Mom will handle it.

Not a minute later, Mom pushes through the kitchen doors.

"What the hell are you serving our guests?" she shouts, charging at Marcy and pressing a coffee mug against her daughter's chest. Inside: black sludge, like dirty motor oil so viscous the spoon doesn't move as Mom swings the mug back and forth. "Why would you do something like this?"

"Mom, I didn't pour that into the mug," Marcy pleads.

"You *saw* me! Remember? You told me to brew another pot. This is *your* coffee."

Her mom pulls back, inspects the mug from a distance. She must believe Marcy. After all, she was right next to her when Marcy was holding a perfectly normal—albeit stale—cup of coffee just moments before serving it.

"Dump it," her mom tells her, handing over the mug. "I'll get a fresh one." Then she slips through the kitchen door without another word.

"Order up!" tonight's sole cook calls.

Marcy plucks the plate out the service window and picks a freshly wrapped set of silverware from a bin at the end of the line. When she brings it out, her mom is already walking away from the table. Marcy can see Grumpy's head ducked over his new mug, examining it as he stirs in artificial sweetener.

Marcy thinks about apologizing but doesn't manifest the thought into action. "Pork roll, egg, and cheese and disco fries," she says, tapping a finger on the edge of the plate three gentle times and whispering something breathlessly while placing his order on the table.

"Excuse me?" Grumpy says.

"Can I get you anything else?"

The man grunts, then takes an enormous bite out of his sandwich. Marcy doesn't waste any time retreating. Behind the counter, she chews her cuticles. On nights like this, Marcy wonders what would happen if she just walked right out of the restaurant, into the thick night air with the bats and the mosquitoes. She doesn't know where she'd even go. And once she's cooled off, how many months, or *years*, would it take to get over the guilt of leaving her mother alone?

She tells herself it isn't worth it. Isn't possible. Daydream, but don't *dream* dream.

A quick, almost imperceptible cough from Grumpy

causes Marcy to look up. She notices him sitting back, holding the remains of his pork roll, egg, and cheese over his plate. His chewing slows, neck cranes toward his sandwich. One beat passes before he slams the sandwich down, spitting chunks of yellow and brown onto the table. Then he uses the flat side of his fork to scrape his tongue, coughing and moaning as he jerks his arm.

It takes Mom a few beats to notice what's going on across the dining room, but when she does, she sprints down the aisle and begins to slap Grumpy's back as he coughs up more bits of food.

Marcy digs deeper into a particularly evasive hangnail. Her eyes don't stray from the coughing man until Mom spins toward her and shouts, "Marcy! *What're you doing?* Get a glass of water!"

She turns around, slides a glass under the fountain, and doesn't remove it until water cascades off the edges. She's too slow for her mom, who hustles over and snatches the glass. Mom nearly waterboards Grumpy as she nurses him. The coughing accelerates. He comes up for air, pushing Mom's arm away from his face. Spurts of water spray with more bits of sandy sludge.

Marcy can't seem to peel her gaze away from the plate of maculated food. The disco fries, only partly touched, swirl below the gravy. An optical illusion that puts Marcy off balance. But she isn't seeing things. Those are no longer disco fries. Even as Marcy steadies herself, the food continues to move, and so do the scraps of pork roll, egg, and cheese.

The man points at the fries, gags, and jumps out of the booth.

Mom apologizes again and again, a broken record of *sorrys*, but Grumpy won't have it. He continues wiping his mouth on a shredded dinner napkin as he spit-shouts, "What is *wrong* with you people? You backwoods guidos!"

Before he kicks open the front door, he catches Marcy staring. His eyes are glossy, flashing from Marcy to Mom and back as he barks, "I'm gonna take you for everything you're worth. You just wait." Then he tucks the napkin back into his mouth and scrubs his tongue while he pushes through the exit.

The restaurant is silent, but there's a steady ringing in Marcy's ears. A blaring of whistles that can't seem to take a breath.

Dennis makes a show of looking at his watch while dropping a few bills onto the table. "I should head out," he tells Mom. "The girls are expecting me."

Mom's silent. Maybe she nods, or maybe she stares blankly. Marcy isn't sure. She can't take her own eyes off the swirling plate of food.

A minute passes, maybe two, before Mom moves. "Marcy…" she starts, using a hand to wipe sweat from her forehead. "It's over."

Marcy glides over to Grumpy's table. His meal, once a sandwich and fries, is an animated Jackson Pollock painting. There aren't any more disco fries on the gray plate—just a knot of writhing strings in sandy mud.

They're flatworms. Long and tan with thin black pinstripes and hammer-shaped heads. Marcy's seen them plenty of times down by the bogs.

And the pork roll isn't pork roll anymore, either. It's… a pile of red insects. Milkweed beetles, to be more specific— black horns like spider legs and crimson exoskeletons shining under the fluorescent lights. They feed on the milkweed flowers of the Pine Barrens.

What was once a slice of gooey yellow American cheese has now shredded into brownish-red discs. Marcy recognizes them as cup fungi. They're all around the Pine Barrens too.

Even the pepper flakes are moving, an infantry of pine beetles marching atop the cup fungi.

The only thing that remained food was the Kaiser roll, baked fresh at an Italian bakery in Runnemede.

Marcy gags, dumping the bugs into a tall trash bin by the register.

Mom rubs both eyes with extended fingers. "That was—Dennis was supposed to… He wanted to invest. In Magissa. Renovate. Change distributors, hire more staff." Mom points a hand at Marcy, then slaps it against her thigh. "You'd get some time off. Maybe me too. But now…" Mom shakes her head, eyes somehow even redder than before. "I hope you're happy."

"What makes you think *I'm* responsible?" Marcy questions.

Mom's eyes are pools. She pushes through the kitchen door one final time tonight and disappears.

Marcy glances at the table and notices the man's Samsung, still face down. She powers it down and tosses it into the trash next to the register before locking the front door. Back at the booth, chunks of soggy bread and mutilated beetles are scattered atop the table. It's an insect Gettysburg after days' long battle.

"Hey," Marcy mutters to herself, "*he* wanted an 'all-Jersey' meal."

She doesn't spend more than a few seconds looking at the mess. She needs to get something before she forgets.

She kneels down next to the booth and lifts the seat—the same seat cushion she had pretended to fluff earlier. With her free hand, she reaches inside and pulls out a russet bag tied with frayed yarn, a black x stitched on its face. It fits in her palm. Without opening it, Marcy can picture exactly what's inside: skeleton of a Pine Barrens tree frog, blood of a Northern Pine snake, pollen of bog asphodel, cicada shell, pokeweed berries, and dried hemlock.

Everything inside this charm bag is indigenous to the area surrounding her family's diner. You get the right quantities, the right conditions—the right *coven*, as Mom calls them—and you've got yourself a protection tool… or, Marcy supposes, a weapon. In case of emergencies.

Is that what tonight was? she wonders.

Marcy is suddenly caught in an undertow of anger, a sensation pulling at her throat. She wants to crush the bag. To scream. She couldn't help herself…

She'd hate to admit that her mom was right, but there's no better word to describe it. *Stupid.*

Mom will read her the riot act when she gets home, once she finishes processing everything. Maybe Mom won't figure out the witchcraft part of it, but there's no one else to take the fall for this mess.

Marcy wonders if she'll ever be allowed to see her friends again, or if she'll be relegated to meet them at the bogs in the dead of night, casting spells under moonlight. She can't believe this one actually worked. She texts the group the details, framing it as a success, but that thread of remorse keeps tugging at her throat. Guilt is woven into her DNA like an ancestral curse, like an unbreakable spell.

If there's a spell to turn food into bugs, there's a way to rewire her circuitry, to get Dennis to reconsider, to spin this yarn into gold. She's sure of it. Now she knows she has the ingredients and the right recipes—and the *cooks* are at the bogs. Maybe they can make nightmares *and* dreams.

We'll take care of this, Marcy thinks. *One all-Jersey meal at a time.*

Early Sunsets
Over Trenton
Zoe Talbot

"....Juicy Joe, Awesome Aaron, Kind Kyla, S.....*sassy* Sarah, and I'm Zany Zoe," I exhale. I've always used "Zany," since my first acrostic poem in third grade. There aren't a whole lot of other things for a "Zoe" to be, at least ones that start with the first letter of my name. The grass is giving me hives, the August sun is unbearable, and the only thing I know for certain about these strangers is that none of them want to be doing icebreakers.

I think I've found the only college in the world that asks what I call breakfast meat, or if a part of their state actually exists, and then responds to your answer with such distaste. Which is kind of crazy, considering you genuinely didn't know that it was an argument people are having. My orientation leaders have flung me into a cultural gauntlet of arbitrary categorization. They've spent the past three days sizing me up, like they don't know whether I'm a Greaser or a Soc. All I can think of right now is how glaringly obvious it is that *I don't belong here.*

This is only somewhat true. It's exciting to be in a new place, a whole twenty-three minutes from home. I'm thrilled to have independence, spend my time studying on the lawn outside my dorm, and all of the other fun things your tour guide tells you about. I guess I just didn't think it would feel like I'm from another realm just because I crossed a state line. I was technically born in Trenton, but I've never lived here. My parents and grandparents have deep roots in the alleged Central Jersey, but I am a dandelion seed who was swept back and forth across the Delaware River.

Meeting new people here makes me sweat. I know this is a common experience among freshmen, but these people are a different breed. Orientation leaders, parents, floormates, it doesn't matter; they are all bloodhounds that can smell that I know how to pump my own gas. Maybe I'm being dramatic, but that's what Snooki would want, right? Is she still relevant? Everything is the end of the world when you're eighteen, anyway. I just don't know why *my* beginning-of-life crisis has to be defined by the fact that I refuse to call it "Italian ice." Reinventing myself is going to be impossible in this microcosm.

By the time my existential crisis has ended, everyone has split off into smaller groups for lunch. I thought that maybe my roommate would want to be friends, as she's from Connecticut, but she's found a group of girls on our floor already. Maybe it's not the out-of-state thing. Maybe I just suck at making friends. Trudging up eight flights of stairs, I call my mom for the third time today. "Homesick" doesn't even begin to cover it.

The light at the end of the tunnel is my first day of class. I crave academic discussion, something objective and stimulating and not based on my zip code. Our desks are in a "U" shape, all looking inwards to facilitate conversation. I'm in Writing 102; leave it to me to be the only English major who tests into writing, especially when all of the non-English majors on my floor didn't. Should I rethink my career before I even start? Add it to the mile-long list of things to worry about.

It's unsustainable to keep pretending to text people on my phone, so my eyes wander. The young man sitting across from me is laughing with his friends. He's already managed to find peers, let alone ones with the same classes. Maybe they know each other from high school, which was another disadvantage of my origins.

My eyes can't stop finding him. He's made up of soft edges; his face is soft and clean-looking, his hair chestnut brown and wispy. He's wearing a graphic tee I can't place. From across the room his eyes aren't entirely clear, but I can tell that they're a warm, deep brown. Something warm settles in my stomach. I can never know exactly how, not even whether it will be positive or not, but I can always tell that someone is going to change my life. He radiates it.

I watch the way he carries himself during class. He's attentive and enthusiastic, especially for a required class. His name is Thomas, he says. His fun fact is that he's forklift certified, even though he's never driven a forklift. I always get carried away in the complicated, unknown lives of strangers. I wonder if Thomas prefers cats to dogs. I wonder if he knows his grandparents. I wonder if he puts cereal or milk first. I like reminders that I am not the center of the universe, and that we are all made up of these little intricacies. I think of how, in all of New Jersey, Thomas found his way to this college, in this section of the class, at this time. Maybe there are worse things than not testing out of Writing 102.

When class is over, his friends swarm out of the room, pulling him away like a grain of sand in the tide. I wonder if we're in the same dorm. As the week passes, I try to catch him again. I begin hanging out a little longer in the dining hall and lingering in the library. Our paths don't cross again until later in the week, when our class meets. We are both early enough to chat - a detail I hadn't realized last week. His friends aren't here yet, probably still fighting off sleep. At the moment, I am bolder than the Zoe I know; my legs move me to the seat next to him until his friends arrive.

"Hi, I'm Zoe," I nod politely. "Just thought I'd say hi,". I've found that one of the cool things about college is that you can just greet strangers without needing a reason. Or is that a Jersey thing too?

"I remember," he nods, "you're the one who likes *Game of Thrones*. Probably the only person who could talk their way out of a circle in this class," he chuckles, but it's not mean. He comes off as realistic without being cruel. Sharp without being dangerous. The details in eyes are clearer now; they're earnest, and soft too, and a little bit more hazel than brown in the right light. "I'm Thomas," he offers.

"But not Tommy," I infer.

"Never Tommy," he confirms.

"I like Thomas better anyway." I say, shrugging. "I've never been the name-shortening type. At the risk of sounding precocious,"

"Didn't think it was." Thomas reassures. "Where are you from?"

The question lingers, like it knows it's dreaded.

"Right over the bridge," I answer for the nth time this week, "Bucks County," I nod. This is the uncharted territory. I never know how much information to give.

"Ah," I watch his wheels turn. "So, Pennsylvania?" Thomas says.

"Yeah, PA." I nod. I wait to feel that clammy feeling on my palms. It never comes.

"Cool," he shrugs.

"Aren't you going to offer your section of Jersey? Whether

you prefer Wawa or Sheetz or whatever?" I tease.

"Oh, you wouldn't know it. No one does, so I usually don't bother. Little town in North Jersey in the middle of nowhere," Thomas waves it off. This surprises me. No pride, barely recognition. Does Thomas care that I say "wooder ice?" It's the taste I need to know - I'm starving.

"What are you doing after class?"

Over sixty orange-adjacent polluted sunsets pass before I finally confess. Thomas has become a welcome staple in my life, and he has warmly opened his friend group up to me. I learn about his three brothers and how he loves his mother. He learns how to make my coffee and the songs I like to play. I proofread his papers, he calculates our tips at the diner. Thomas and classes are the only constants in my life, but I haven't been completely honest with him. The secret gnaws at me each day. I need to tell someone. I need to tell him.

We're sitting in his stupid little square car that I hate, but I'd never complain about. Driving in Jersey is something I've gotten better at, but still frustrates me. Why can't I make a left turn from where I just came from? Why do we have to reinvent the wheel just to "improve the flow of traffic?"

Thomas hums softly as he pulls into one of the gas stations on the corner, and the smell of diesel hits me. The October air is the perfect amount of chilly. Despite what I'm about to profess, I've never felt more at home.

"Can I ask you something?" I turn from the window towards him.

"Yeah?" he tilts his head, as if he's unsure what could possibly be following such a daunting request. It is now or never. I am a dam bursting at the seams.

"How do you… do this?" I lean over in the passenger seat, motioning my hands vaguely. His eyebrows furrow. For the first time ever, I am at a loss for words.

"Drive? Get gas?" he pauses. "Talk to a person?" Thomas clarifies.

"It sounds dumb when you put it like that," I sigh. Maybe I've made a dire mistake. "But I've never done it before, and I'm scared, but I trust you, so I thought maybe… you'd show me?" I propose. He handles me like a million girls have asked him how to ask someone else to pump their gas.

"Watch this," he smiles, rolling down the window. "Twentyregularcash," he says, handing over a bill. It sounds like it's all one word, a secret code uttered for resources, but the man begins to fill the car. I feel as if I've infiltrated an underground society.

"That easy?" I grimace.

"That easy," he nods.

"But that requires waiting for a person, and then talking to that person, and then more waiting. I can do it in half the time, with none of the anxiety," I argue. "There is a reason this is the only state that requires this," I slump back in the passenger seat. Another learning curve. "We're creating a power dynamic that we don't need." I look out the window, brooding. Even if I finally understand, I do not need to enjoy it.

"Wait, haven't you gotten gas since you got to school?" Thomas chuckles in disbelief, nodding in acknowledgement as the attendant closes the gas tank. Just like when we met, he has the air about him that is honest, but not mean.

"So…no," I look down at my lap, "I do it when I visit home," I shrug. "I don't drive enough to make it inconvenient, but I've been living in Jersey for months now, and I've still never *not* pumped it. I felt like it was too late for me to ask, which I know sounds so dumb because it's so self-explanatory. Like, *yes*, in practice, I totally could have just been grown up and done it, but the idea of just showing up was so horrifying," I sigh. "Anxiety is no one's friend,"

"I get it," Thomas says. "But really, you get used to it," he assures, pulling back onto the road. To me, a weight has just been lifted. A seal broken. He doesn't know how intimate the ritual he just performed is. It really is such a stupid point of tension between me, myself, and I, but something so functional should not seem so daunting to the adult I supposedly am.

"As if you've known anything else," I deflect. He pauses for a moment, and the car hangs in silence.

"Is that what you think?" he asks. My brain scours for what that could possibly mean.

"What?"

"Zo, I'm not from New Jersey," Thomas says with a little smile like it's something I was told but forgot, not an earth-shattering revelation.

"You're literally from North Jersey," I recall.

"Ish. You asked for what part of Jersey I'm from, I gave it. But I'm not really *from* here. I grew up in Maryland," Thomas keeps his eyes on the road, but his sly smile reveals how much he's enjoying himself.

"Shut up," I demand, my world distorted. The last two months of my life have been a lie.

"One of us was born in New Jersey, and it was not me,"

Thomas confirms.

"Wait, your great-grandfather literally worked on the *Trenton Makes* bridge. You're, like, Jersey royalty or something," I recall, trying to make sense of his origins.

"Right, and all my grandparents grew up in Maryland, and then when I was seven, we made our way back here. Just like you," Thomas glances over, as if this should be an obvious solution to my distress.

"You're my Garden State guru, and you're not even from here?" my jaw slacks.

"Okay, so that is totally not a real thing," Thomas says pointedly, "but if it were, being 'from somewhere' is arbitrary. I've lived here for over a decade. By the end of college, you'll have lived here four years. You'll be just as much of an expert as me." He parks in the damp, dimly lit parking garage. The cars are an audience, a packed venue, even though I'm certain they're all empty this time of day. "You don't owe it to anyone to make yourself into something you aren't. I know it feels polarizing now, but that's just because you're sharing that part of yourself over and over and over. Every freshman feels that way. Some just have a little bit more of a home field advantage than others." he relaxes in his seat, now unbuckled and turned towards me. "New Jersey loves you, Zo. You just have to let it,"

"Alright, alright. Thank you," I chuckle. It's a silly thing to think about, but there's little room to judge as the person who almost cries over asking for fuel. Thomas reaches across the center console, taking my hand. His thumb rubs my hand absentmindedly. He holds more affection in his thumb than some men I've dated hold in their whole bodies. Something shifts in my chest, and that warm feeling comes back. I understand now.

"Anything for you," Thomas smiles. There's a door. I feel myself rushing through it.

"Can I kiss you ?" I ask softly, meeting his eyes. In my gaze, he finds my second confession of the hour. In lieu of an answer, Thomas leans forward, catching my lips with his. Our union is brief and sweet, and he tastes like the mango smoothies we got earlier. I recall from an earlier conversation that it's his first; I'm gracious he's trusted me with such a thing. It's so tender that I almost forget we're in this musty garage. He kisses me again, still holding my hand. Maybe I finally get what "If I Should Fall Behind" is about. We smile into each other's lips a bit longer.

"Okay, one more question," I say quietly. "And nothing fuel-related, I promise," it makes him chuckle.

"Yeah, shoot. Anything," Thomas spurs me on.

"Did you know that George R.R. Martin is from New Jersey?" I nudge him with my elbow, shamelessly impressed with myself. "A lot of the Targaryen stuff is actually based on-"

"Bayonne," he finishes. I am beyond enamored. "Has a lot to do with the rise and fall of his own origins, if I remember,"

"Look at you. A master of analysis," I grin. If there's anything that can win my heart, it's a witty brunette who knows his literature.

"I have a *really* good writing tutor," Thomas shrugs nonchalantly, pulling my hand to his lips gently. I hope we get to stay in this golden moment a while longer.

Platinum Platypus
Matt Lydon

PLATINUM PLATYPUS
STORY & ART by MATT LYDON

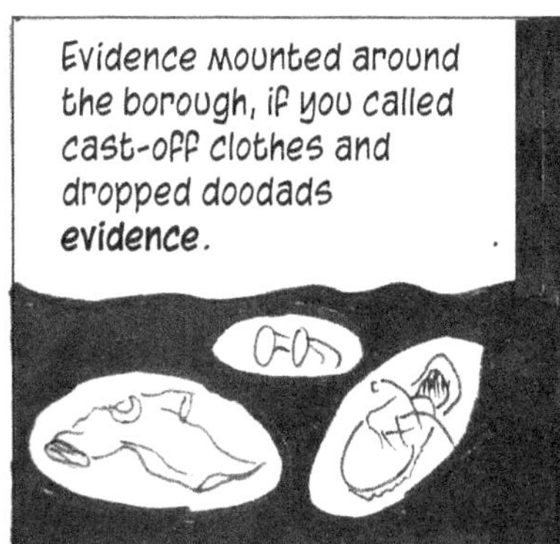
Evidence mounted around the borough, if you called cast-off clothes and dropped doodads evidence.

When a barely regarded neighbor vanishes, it generally doesn't ping your social radar...

...but the popular cheer captain?
CHEE
Well, THAT just tore at the very fabric of the town!

So the townies organized a search party.
EAT AT THE PLAT

They found nothing that first night, except Sadie's pom-poms.

Days turned into weeks...
OCTOBER

...and SEARCHERS began vanishing.

The mayor forbid the local paper from reporting on the story...
No.

...but that didn't stop the bloggers!
I BET it's the Jersey Devil!
BELIEVE

One night a team of cryptid hunters showed up. You could hear laughing all the way across the field into the parking lot of the Platinum Platypus. Until, that is, their leader, Agnes, asked a question.

In the shadow of a big silver maple tree that had been overlooked during the previous outings, the search party came across a cache of bones. Were these bones of the neighbors and search party volunteers who disappeared? Were Sadie's remains in that charnel pile? Either way, the bones were clean of flesh, but dark and slick like a just finished hot wing.

What the party didn't know, that whatever had done all this...
...was still watching.
I
WAS
WATCHING

In fact...
...they never saw me coming until...
IT WAS TOO LATE

I AM NOT OF EARTH.
I AM DEATH INCARNATE.
I AM PLATYPUS
I AM DESTROYER
YOU... ARE FOOD.
End

Hotel Pool
Traffic Cone
Itua Uduebo

The broken gate door didn't inspire much confidence. It was the first thing I noticed getting out of the car, besides the genuine sea air smell. The lock was intact, the important part, but three of the iron bars were missing the top half. Functional but deeply defective, which is how I felt about my better judgment the more I took in the hotel accommodations.

Four floors of rooms spread across a front-facing section and two wings on the side. An unappealing paint selection of blue-grey for the wood siding and a dark roof, like the ocean inverted. A crystal-blue pool that was too small for a proper sized party and too big for the front space of the compound. The doors all looked needlessly ornate and the fuck-ton of domed security cameras gave the impression of a half-baked panopticon.

Not a small building, just the right amount of bed to keep the rent paid on this corner of Seaside Heights. Close enough to the beach and the boardwalk that even the laziest long-weekend day drinkers would be able to navigate. Far enough from the nice, already-rented beach houses that no one lame enough to call the cops on noise violations would be affected. It was perfect for a kind of guest—just not the guest I was expecting to be. But I should've known better.

"Still can't believe we ended up booking this converted mental asylum," I remarked while pulling my bags from the trunk. "Yo, Curtis, where's the other bag with the gravity bong?"

"It's the green one, with the stripes and shit," he replied, "sorry, Kola, gimme a sec, I have to look up the entry code for our room again."

"Aren't they already in there?"

"Nah, they went to the store to get some groceries. Brian and Pauly are getting shit for the grilling, Joey's at the liquor store. Let them know if you want anything in the group chat. Tonight we're getting pizza."

It was fun to be part of a detour from the routine. Curtis had told me it was the eighth time he and his hometown friends had done their Memorial Day weekend trip to Long Beach Island, and I had been given the honor of the first outsider to get an invite. I'd met the guys before, I liked them enough, and obliterated enough Coors to earn my way into the party. It was cool to be asked somewhere on a boys' weekend, a social feature that had been very absent from an over sheltered childhood and some missed opportunities in college. It was a Friday off work that I desperately needed, a few dozen beers I was ready to get through, and ten other guys I'd be getting to know.

I was excited to come, even after I was told that we were actually going to Seaside instead of LBI because of Curtis's dreadful scheduling. I was still excited when I saw the first picture of the hotel and was told that the main attraction of Seaside during MDW was the local Jersey teens flocking the town for after-prom weekend. I was even still, somehow, excited when I learned about the motel. And then we opened the door.

It wasn't a true shit-hole, that would have been better. When something is horrible you can justify any response — you can cancel the trip and go home, you can book a super expensive second option, you can get into a huge passive aggressive fight to distract from the roaches in the toilet or hole in the ceiling. It wasn't a hovel or even particularly dirty, no health hazards. Nothing was dying except my sense of taste.

Dire. That's the word. Absolutely fucking dire.

Unwieldy beige tiles covering every inch of the floor's surface area, directly under a crusty, white-paneled roof. Two couches that seemed intentionally selected to produce the worst combination of lukewarm salmon and pine green checked pattern. A Victorian-era, blond wood dining table with non-descript chairs that had already been moved to make room for beer pong, which explained the empty cooler that had been positioned as a coffee table in front of the pink couch. A Bush-era television mounted at a doctor's waiting room height with one straggling iPhone charger dangling from the open outlet.

Even the good parts were bad. Each piece of wall art looked like it cost more than the entire furniture set under it, and the biggest ones were triple the size of the TV and both in the smallest bedroom. The bathroom was incredibly well lit in a way that made the rest of the place seem darker.

All the bedrooms, at least, were free of any bugs, visible stains, or weird outlets. Large enough to accommodate barely-unpacked suitcases, inevitable laundry piles, and sets of two and three men in their mid-twenties figuring out the most heterosexual sleeping arrangements possible. Curtis and I were already slated for bed-sharing, mostly because it would have been cruel to pair me with a quasi-stranger, and partially because I was his designated "make sure he doesn't drown this weekend" watcher. Easier to know if he got arrested if I'm the one expecting to hear his snoring.

The two best rooms had already been taken, but ours

had the most interesting wall painting, so it wasn't a bad pick. Something I could stare at in the hungover morning to calm the tequila in my skull. I took my side of the bed and laid down for a few minutes of peace before the impending calamity. I was excited to be making new friends, to be seeing a place that I'd only known from four seasons of watching *The Jersey Shore* in middle school. A little taste of a different life, the essence of any travel.

The rest of the guys came pouring in over the next few hours, back from their store runs with a small mountain of processed food, cheap alcohol, smoking paraphernalia and all-American beach nonsense. At some point I knew all their names, I committed to making friends with Curtis's friends for Curtis's sake. We were found brothers from the earliest days of prep school football and these guys had known him even longer, that mattered to me. After a while they kind of faded, but I remembered the moments that counted, the elation and braindead happiness of being free and young and on break from post-grad reality.

That first night was an inundation into the lives and times of the Pleasantville social scene; who fucked whose sister, whose party that guy got into a fight at, which friend from high school had an overdose that the family tried to hide. An unintentional oral history of a slice of white America that I felt more comfortable hearing about from afar. Escalating volume levels over the college rap playlists and screaming over violated beer pong rules. Once the delivery pizzas had been devoured and the last six guys awake starting debating which NBA highlight reel to put on the ludicrous television, it felt like it was time for bed. I didn't need predictive powers to see that I'd need to load up on sleep for the weekend to come.

With a surprisingly light hangover, I got up at my usual early time to take advantage of a bathroom that hadn't been too defiled by eleven other men. The first day of the Memorial Day Weekend was always beach day, the two-to-seven hours where a combination of weather conditions, crowdedness, and sentiment on public drinking laws determined if you were going to make summer memories or just increase your odds of skin cancer. It had been years since the last time I'd had a serious beach day, one weekend a college girlfriend had taken me on. I'd spent the whole time panicking about not getting an internship so I might've missed out on the sweet sun and waves. To ensure a good, calm day I'd also come equipped with edibles that were still very much illegal at the time, and enough for several repeats depending on their effects.

The rest of the crew woke up over the morning and I was treated to a new culinary experience: ordering a Taylor Ham breakfast sandwich, being corrected and told it's a pork roll, then watching four men spend the next twenty minutes arguing after we'd already put the order in. Both sides did a good job, but I ended up siding on the Taylor Ham side because pork roll just reminded me too much of a 2000s nu-rock band name to take seriously.

Despite the name controversy the sandwich and iced coffee were a perfect start, and pretty soon we had the morning round of beer tasting going. Someone wanted to go out, someone said it was too early. There's always cross-talk and debates in a large group but it felt like some of them were arguing just to argue. That little bit of danger that a series of verbal fights can turn into legitimate violence is the secret spice of any healthy male friendship dynamic. As an impartial observer, it was interesting getting to see the push-and-pull between the young adult men figuring out beach logistics and the teenage children holding on to unspoken grievances.

Curtis and I had a bit of that too, but in our case all of his offenses were so deeply amusing that I had no choice but to forgive him more each time I remembered one. I don't know what he'd say if you asked him about shit I did to him, but it would probably boil down to something stupid I only did because of a blood-alcohol-content level that he had caused.

Eventually we left, and eventually the sun was perfectly exposed over the sand. The local population of families who'd spent two hours in traffic, dealt with the parking situation, and had to purchase some kind of barbaric "beach pass" ticket was scattered across a mosaic of bright towels and umbrellas. There were kids running around playing the usual oceanside games, teens loitering and socializing with the societally permitted levels of ogling. People reading, tanning, sleeping, and a few guys taking long swigs of "water" bottles and passing them around.

The gummy I'd taken after my horribly early game of beer pong was in full swing. Each sun ray felt like it was working a particular patch of skin, baking away all the substances in my blood. Everything was brighter and louder, the sand was eternal. It was a heat dream that I was drowning inside.

On a very stupid whim, I decided to take my exploration into the water. The drastic change from the warmth to the ice-cold first impact was a tear in space-time. I felt the pull from the tide, not the deep ripping and thrashing of the currents, just the light tug that we use for our recreation. It kept taking me by surprise each time.

A girl ran by me, then a bunch of her friends. I recognized them from outside our hotel suite the night before, some of the high school seniors crowding our accommodations and making Curtis's efforts funnier by the minute. They looked so happy, so completely overjoyed to be in this place at this time in their lives. I couldn't remember the last time I thought I felt like that—the last time I felt like everything in front of me would always be exactly, completely good, forever.

It felt stupid feeling old at that age, when I was on that beach trip with that amount of weed and booze in my system, but it occurred to me that I was chasing a façade. I'd never feel like that again, I'd never be that young again. A boys' weekend at the Jersey Shore was a Xerox of a euphoria that I'd only barely scratched a few times in college.

Something in me died in that water.

Nothing sad, nothing that robbed me of happiness. Just some delusion over how far back in time a good experience can take you. I decided that if I was never going to get that feeling back, then I needed to find something new.

I got out and needed to dry myself, needed to recover from all the sensations. One of the guys had taught me an innovative method for public urination where you make a little hole in the sand, whip it out right in there, do your business and execute a seamless tuck-and-roll-over. Once I'd pulled off that classy maneuver, I packed up my beach items and walked back to the house with two of the others.

The suite filled up man by man and the beers resumed their mandated flow. Guys started coming in and out of the room with freshly prepared grill food from the communal setup by the pool. I needed every bite I could get, knowing that while I'd been having epiphanies, Curtis was dreaming of the night's disasters.

As soon as the sun started to set, I could feel the tentacles start to wrap around me. With this many guys it was always a question of who wants to go where, which bars are even good, and inevitably a bunch of people preferring to drink at home. With him, those questions simply didn't exist: we were going, we were going to all of them that had at least one attractive woman inside, and we wouldn't be back home until our wallets and endocrine systems were damaged.

It was the brother's code: no tequila shot left behind, no game left unattempted. I can sit here and say a million things about how he dragged me around, how he was always the crazy one, how he was the textbook definition of a bad influence.

I can say all that and it would all be true but the more important truth is that I fucking loved it. I was a stereotype melange: immigrant kid with strict parents that becomes a partier mixed with Black boy in a white school syndrome. (In later years I'd work through those identity and childhood issues through therapy, but this was the mid 2010s so that was still off the table). I craved his freedom, his complete commitment to personal satisfaction, and that craving became an understanding that became a lifelong friendship. Assuming we lived long enough to make that mean something.

That first night was nothing: not a bad night, not a shitty time, just nothing. Oblivion for oblivion's sake. Every bar was the same as the one before, the same carbon copy characters and over-the-top lighting. If I had convinced myself that my

MTV memories of Seaside Heights nightlife were exaggerated, every guy in a tank top dripping with East European cologne and every girl with a shitty spray tan and short shorts was bringing me back to clarity.

Going out in the city was always an exercise in financial and mating frustration, but the local crowd was more designed to challenge comprehension.

How many pairs of indoor sunglasses is enough for the strobe lights to be classified as solar?

Can society evolve past the need for tropical fishbowl cocktails the size of small Ottomans?

If a girl starts dancing on top of a bar table and takes her shirt off, but no one is around to throw dollars at her, did it even happen?

And lastly, and definitely most importantly, do the Chainsmokers and Mike Posner and Calvin Harris actually exist or did the government invent that music to increase the party economy and, by proxy, the birthrate?

All valid questions, all running through the fragments of my mind that were left after the fifth Long Island Iced Tea. When I was well past the point of being coherent enough to attempt talking to any women, I stumbled around the bar until I found Curtis blacked out in the backyard of the bar splitting cigarettes with two grown men who looked like they were coming by to collect that week's kick. Being a fan of *The Sopranos* myself, I chatted with our new friends for a while before pulling Curtis away and getting a very bumpy Uber. One of the guys who stayed behind had ordered some late night fast food to the house, and I took the courtesy of bringing an embarrassing amount of chicken wings and fries to bed for a drunken movie and a meal. The first thirty minutes of *The Dark Knight* are always worth it.

Eight hours later, I woke up to a nightmare.

Not the hangover that was threatening my belief in the Earth being stable, or the stomach that was flowing with regrets. The horrid realization that I was about to be trapped in a zoo.

When it rains like a monsoon on the last full day of your weekend beach trip, it means a couple of things. There's no illusion that the day is going to change, no chance of salvaging a couple of hours of sunshine. Everyone gives up immediately on having a day outside and starts to wonder how the next ten hours before the last night out are going to go.

If we were a more civilized bunch, in a living space with enough room for separation, something better might have happened. Maybe a few guys would've had a movie marathon, someone could've done some reading, a few board games could've come into the mix.

Instead, we embarked on a ten-hour descent into the pits of male behavior. It didn't start out bad; spirits were high, everyone was having a friendly time. The boys at home for a day, eating some breakfast, talking about the night before, catching up on some more bullshit from back home. Everything was going great, all before a friendly set of pre-lunch drinking games turned into multiple hours of sustained alcohol consumption. By the end of that we'd dropped all the pretext of keeping score, and that's when it took a turn.

I'd drank just to drink before, but I'd never drank out of sheer fucking boredom. That idea that you're doing something stupid to kill your brain is fun, but inhaling a poison simply because you'd rather feel nothing than feel the need to talk to the guy next to you is a bad feeling.

As the day progressed, the tone, the conversations, charged. More snide remarks, more offensive jokes, more deeply personal and needlessly embarrassing stories coming up about hook-up mishaps and fuck-ups from school days. Meaningless debates about the moral character of certain local figures. Slurs of all flavors and manner being tossed around with intent to provoke, including a couple of lighter remarks my way from my least favorite member of the group. I would like to say I responded appropriately but I probably made things worse and much more immature — thankfully he was a lot smaller than me so it was irrelevant.

The worst of it all was the goddamn icing - a truly idiotic pastime born from frat blogs from the 2000s. For those of you who had better friends in your life: the purpose of the game is to hide a bottle of cotton candy-sweet street wine in a place where the first person that finds it has to chug the entire thing. It's funny the first time, a harmless prank. The fifth time it's annoying. After the tenth icing of that day, the eleventh instance was pretty much destined to a blind-drunk screaming session with grabbed shirts and direct threats.

That was the point when I realized I was just the calmest gorilla in the cage, a little less enthusiastic in my prodding and poking but right there with them, desperate to see it. That moment when all the rules and demands of society fade away and things tip over into raw expression. It was the other side of freedom and forgetting inhibition, the negative logical endpoint.

No punches were thrown, of course, because punches

never go between friends. You don't really want to kill the people you've known your entire life over ten minutes of drunk pranking. Half-apologies were offered, more beers were consumed, and finally, by the grace of God, it was time to hit the boardwalk.

I've been stunned before in my life, very few times. Most of them involved the first time watching classic movies or certain albums. Once it was at the aquarium the first time I saw a dolphin in person, and another at the Griffith Observatory at exactly the right time of sunset. Being on that boardwalk, feeling the color splash all over me from the bright signs. All the day's stupor and slog wiped away by this carnival atmosphere, the rides and the games, families searching for fun and nightlife wanderers seeking the next distraction.

It felt like this was the "something" I'd felt like chasing in that ocean water. Wonder and brightness and the energy of a crowd of people off to the next attraction. Maybe youth could be replaced by pure visual distraction, by enough nights in enough beautiful places that the struggles of all the other days just means less. Enough funnel cakes and Tilt-a-Whirls to make the noises go away.

We were aimless but focused, seeking out the next high. Curtis had taken a detour to get a temporary tramp stamp plastered across his tailbone, and one of the boys had picked up a citation for public drinking. Both impressive acts of impulsive stupidity, but nothing to disrupt our night. I decided I needed a little calorie load and took a detour to a hot dog joint, telling the crew I'd catch up with them at the next stop in the group chat.

She came at me from the side, stumbling in and bumping

the slightest shoulder graze.

I noticed her immediately, noticed the long black hair and boldly sized gold earrings. Beautiful and loud and smiling through her yelling. An accent that had only registered at that level of attractiveness the first time I saw Lorraine Bracco in *Goodfellas*. She didn't even take sight of me as she dictated a long order for a large crew that I could see waiting outside the store.

It was one of those "blink and you'll miss it" type of situations. I knew what I wanted, I could see it there, and if I didn't say the first clever thing that came to mind, she'd be gone and I'd be there waiting for a warm weiner.

"And get the lady some extra fries too, on me."

OK, so it was more "extraordinarily generous" than clever, but I was legitimately intoxicated at that point. The fact that she said "thank you" and looked at me long enough to register faint interest was enough reward.

When I asked her name she told me, "Francesca but everyone calls me Frankie," and when I started asking a much dumber question she saved me by asking if I wanted to get one of the burgers she'd ordered. Tacit invitation to sit with her and her friends to eat, all a friendly bunch, all out-of-towners coming in from Philly for the long weekend. It took me exactly three comments about the Eagles to earn an honorary spot in the night's plans, and another sweet look from Frankie. They could have told me they wanted to go to a Siberian prison camp and I would've followed in a heartbeat.

I let the Pleasantville boys know I was headed to the big nightclub, The Bamboo Bar, and they could meet up with me. If they responded anything back to me then it didn't register.

We walked and talked and Frankie looked like a neon angel in her pink crop top and baby blue shorts.

She asked me about New York and I asked her about Philly and we both knew we weren't talking about the thing we were talking about. Bodies in silent conversation, observing lips and eyes and looks. Lines of politeness being tiptoed over, with each risqué comment getting a little quieter, away from prying eyes. Everyone she'd brought knew the game that was happening in the back of our little convoy, and that only made it better. I'm sure at least one of the guys there was pissed about it, and that made it better in a way that years of therapy will never be able to undo.

Once we were inside the club, once we were drowning in the music and three of those monumental fishbowl cocktails, the dancing sealed the deal. The silent conversation had ended and now we were in thrall, letting hips and impaired judgment decide everything else. She knew how to move, and I knew how to press my luck. I learned where she wanted to be touched, where she wanted me to hold, where she'd let me plant my lips on her neck. Her friends had scattered, off to run around in the unending night, seeking their own carnal discussions.

After one particularly stirring song, she leaned her head back and told me everything with her eyes. I caressed her chin, kissed her deeply, and continued until the whole planet melted away. It could all have ended right there: the rapture, the nuclear missiles, the worldwide plague that would come just two short years in the future. Nothing else would've mattered.

We got wilder and less aware of surroundings, right in the middle of a dance floor where the amount of groping per square foot had gone far above the levels of good taste. I had already lost the part of my mind that considered the fact that I couldn't take her back to my place, that there was really no way I'd get invited to hers, that I'd have to make some desperate, disgusting proposal to ravish her in some alley or the club bathroom. I couldn't afford to think that far ahead. She was responding to all my unspoken questions, and I could feel that something was going to explode soon.

We took a pause, stared into each other, and then she grabbed my hand and led me to one of the large lounge booths on the side of the dance floor. She straddled me tightly, popping the top button of her shorts. My hands unbuckled my belt by instinct and gave her the room to slip her hand in. With an instant realization, I reciprocated. She found me, I found her.

We stayed wrapped in each other, to keep the arm movements out of view and the warmth of each other's bodies close. Raw movement, pure need.

She shook in small waves when it started to hit her, when my practiced technique came in handy. My journey ended in a lot less elegant fashion, mostly all over the left side of my shirt. She did me the incredible stuff to pick some of it in her finger and give me a perfectly erotic taste-test send-off.

We re-clothed ourselves, completely back in reality. The aftermath of increasingly rash and hilariously successful choices. She gave me a little ego-boosting compliment and I asked if she'd want a more intimate demonstration. Maybe part of her wanted to, maybe she'd gotten what she needed and I was already turning into a funny memory, but she felt alright with giving me her phone number as a "maybe later."

Once we were out of the booth, once we were back with the people and there were friends to be found and beds to be slept in, once we realized that we would probably never see each other ever again, the only thing that felt appropriate was for me to stay until she was safely back with her group, and for me to make my way home.

The lights on the boardwalk were dimmer. Possibility and potential replaced by certainty of destination. I would be walking home, and then I'd be in bed. The other guys had gone to a different bar, citing the outrageous cover charge that I had been way too horny to even notice I paid for her, myself, and two of her girlfriends.

If that was the "something," if the unending, insatiable lust for satisfaction was going to be what replaced my dead youth, then I was ready to embrace eternal struggle and temporary perfection. I could do this forever: pursue, acquire, chase. A lot of things on the list, but women above all else, the sweetest fruit. If I could feel like *that* even a fraction of the time, then everything else was worth it.

The boardwalk ended, the dimly lit streets were emptied, and the broken gate was inside. I was all ready to go in when I noticed that the lone man in the pool wasn't one of the high school drunks or a random old man.

"Why the fuck are you still awake, Curtis?"

"Yooooo, Kola! Get your sweet chocolate ass in here, man. Beer and cigs over there if you want some."

It was stupid. It was stupid to be drunk in a pool, and it was stupid to be up at 3 AM when we had to wake up the next morning and help clean up. But it was also my last night on the Shore, so I stripped down, supplied myself, and submerged into the water.

I told him about my escapades at the Bamboo Bar, to which he expressed pride in getting some action but disappointment that I wasn't currently making a half-Italian-half-Nigerian baby. When I asked where I should propose to have this lovemaking, he told me, and I quote, "There's always a dumpster somewhere."

He told me about the rest of his night, about who threw up and who almost got thrown out of the bar and who was definitely cheating on their girlfriend with a bar girl right now. Curtis, the natural storyteller, made it sound like they'd all had a bit of the magic that night. He himself had gotten too drunk to score any girls but he had three waiting back in the city for him so I didn't exactly feel too bad.

When we were all done chatting, when it was silent except for the beer can swishing and cigarettes cackling, I confessed those feelings I'd had at the beach. That sense that something was over after this weekend, and that the next thing would probably be better but I just didn't know what it was yet. And how much it worried me.

He didn't say anything for a while, and then he spoke to me.

"Honestly man, I don't think that's how life works. Like, yeah, sure you get older and youth ends, and some bullshit starts and then it doesn't end until you're in the ground. But that's just time, you know? It's not *you*. You don't need to replace yourself with anything. Getting through the day, getting through the horror show, and finding something to smile about and maybe someone to share it with? That's all life is. You don't need to find the next 'thing' because being happy and free isn't a thing that ends, it's a choice you can try and make every day. And on the days you can't, you get through them the best you can, with whatever helps you cope, and then you try again the next day. Everything else? It's all noise, man. Noise and bright lights."

It was silent for a bit after that. We didn't need to say anything else. There was a whole future left for talking, and this wasn't part of it.

Our silence was broken by a pack of returning teenagers. A stampede of hormones and summer vacation plans and dreams. One of them, a boy with curly blonde hair, ran past the gate dragging a traffic cone behind him. His friend, a young Black boy with a recognizable face, begging him not to do the inevitable.

Maybe he saw us, maybe he's just a great drunk athlete, but when he launched it into the pool we had the benefit of being out of the splash zone. He barely even broke stride, barely stopped to admire his amazingly pointless act of vandalism. There were more drinks to have, more girls to chase, more mid-cranial-development memories to make; this random act of petty theft wouldn't even register by the end of the hour.

I stared at the thing, bobbing in the water, out of place and adrift. I laughed, then stopped, then laughed again. A warm pool, a loud place, a good friend, and a bright orange reminder that things end when they end. Found in the water, and never lost again.

Seaside
NJ
Heights
NO DIVING
4 FT

Spinning Wheel Diner in Lebanon is my favorite diner. Right from its glowing neon and chrome exterior, you know you're in for a memorable experience. Staff are always friendly, and every meal I have--whether breakfast, lunch, or dinner--is enjoyable.

~Patrick Lombardi (*All-Jersey Meal*)

To be from New Jersey is to have a diner for all occasions. Late night college dinners/early breakfast at the Parkway Diner near TCNJ, lunch with my grandmother at the Rainbow Diner in Brick, post-Shop Rite shift meals at the Toms River Diner (or TRD)... wherever you are in the state, at whatever time, there was a shiny metallic beacon ready to feed you. Every place had their own disco fries, but if they aren't completely loaded with gravy and cheese and need to be eaten with a fork, do they even count as NJ disco fries?

~S. Atzeni (*Jimmie Leeds is a Bad Friend*)

Tops Diner - but I am a disco fry purist. Brown Gravy, Mozzarella.

~Alicia Cook (*The (Garden State) Waitress*)

Favorite Diner

I love an autumn drive through Hollow Road. I think it's in Montgomery Township, coursing along tranquil woods, a babbling brook, historic residences, and a hilly landscape skirting the Sourland Mountain Preserve.

~Scott Napolitano (*How The Story Ends*)

Favorite drive: Perth Amboy waterfront

~ Apara Mahal Sylvester (*Let's Play Ball!*)

I spend a lot of time driving North Rt 23 through rural Sussex -- there's a particular hilltop, on an old dirt road, where locals gather from miles around, rain or shine, for good company and a chance of seeing a stellar sunset.

~ J. E. Krantz (*Meditations of a Hiker*)

My grandmother used to share stories of Trenton when she was young, how it was the place to be. A lot has changed in the past seventy years, but when you follow State Street over through Historic Trenton there are moments where you can still see that spark that made it such a hot spot back in the day.

~The Unforgiving Loop (*Writing on the Walls*)

Best Scenic Drives

Route 30
Danny Garrett

US 30 would take us all the way there. No directions needed. "You'll know it's close when you see the glow on the horizon," was what I'd said to her an hour before. Now she was chewing gum with her reading light on and I had my window cracked so that the sound of the wind on the one side and her chewing on the other side had me in a trance. Time was rolling right along. My hands and feet were doing the driving just fine on their own, so my brain took a trip to 1991. That was actually the last time I'd *been* to Atlantic City. It was Summertime. I had that little Honda CB350 then. Man, that bike could move. And the girls liked it, too. It was the shape, I think. It had kind of a European shape to it. It was the kind of bike you'd see in a movie about Europe or something. All of a sudden the chewing stopped. The book was closed in her lap.

"Shouldn't we be going East?"

"We are going East," I said.

"That sign said 30 West."

"What sign?"

"A *sign*," she said, "on a post with numbers and letters. It said 30 *West*."

"We must have turned the wrong way out of that gas station."

"When you *had* to have a Mallomar. That was half an hour ago, Paul."

"You're sure about the sign?"

"Look, that's the burger stand we stopped at an hour ago. You'd have driven us all the way back to Philadelphia if I didn't look up just now."

I braked and turned into the dirt lot of the burger stand

and turned us around facing Route 30. My finger lifted the turn signal lever and my foot pressed the pedal down and we were headed East.

"We'll need gas," she said.

"I know a place," I said.

Then the book opened up again and the chewing started again. That was the other nice thing about the motorcycle. You never cared if you got lost. You'd just ride along until you saw a sign for the turnpike or the parkway or somewhere and you'd figure it out. Sometimes you'd find a new road that way, or a bar. Man, what was the name of that place on 73? Anyway, I think I ought to think about getting another bike before the years start to catch up with me. That CB could really move. And the shape of it, too.

Northwood Meadows:
Plus+
Andy Chang

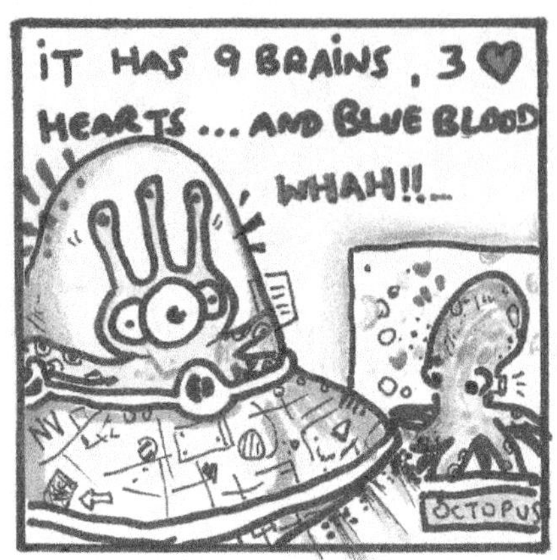
IT HAS 9 BRAINS, 3 HEARTS... AND BLUE BLOOD WHAH!!...
OCTOPUS

..YOU ARE AN AWESOME ALIEN!...
LET'S SHAKE... HANDS!!

...THAT'S MY LEG!!
ANDY CHUNG // AUG. 26, 2023
NORTHWOOD MEADOWS ©

I DONNO!

NORTHWOOD MEADOWS
ANDY SHAMA // AUG. 26. 2023

WHAT IS ON THE...
DARK SIDE OF THE
MOON?

YOU MEAN THE FAR
SIDE?
OF
THE MOON!!
IT'S SIDE'B ON PINK
FLOYD'S ROCK ALBUM!
WHAH?
NORTHWOOD MEADOWS ©
ANDY CHANG // AUG. 20,23'

...WE WERE LOOKING ...
FOR A VACATION SPOT.

NORTHWOOD MEADOWS ©

AMY CHANG // APR 2. 2023

Let's Play Ball!

Apara Mahal Sylvester

John Sylvester was born on September 2, 1954 in Bound Brook, New Jersey. He was the second of three children born to Sophie and Francis (Frank) Sylvester. Sophie was the first female business owner in town and was the proprietor of Beauty Lounge on Main Street. Frank, aka "The Chief," was the Chief of Police.

As early as John could walk, he took a liking to baseball. John's father bought him all types of baseball equipment from Whiffle balls to hard balls and bats.

Baseball ran in the family. John's father, Frank, was a catcher and also learned the sport at a young age, and passed on what he knew to his son John by practicing with him daily in their backyard.

As John grew older, he graduated from the backyard to the field of Memorial Park. John wanted to be like Mickey Mantle, so he played center field, just like "The Mick" did.

John's dad took him to the park daily to teach him how to catch, pitch, throw and hit. All the neighborhood children played in the park, and they used to watch John and his dad play baseball. In third grade, John recalled that he was playing baseball with the eighth graders at Robert Morris School. Coach McGloughlin, Physical Education teacher and coach at the school, allowed John to play baseball with the seventh and eighth graders. The older children didn't mind having such a young boy on their team. All the kids wanted to do was play baseball.

The neighborhood children used to love to watch The Chief practice infield and outfield drills with John at Memorial Park. Hours of hitting fly balls to John and his older brother Frankie. The neighborhood kids enjoyed being in the outfield catching balls during John's batting practice. Once, John hit a ball so high and far that it landed several backyards away.

John attended Bound Brook High School. During his freshman year, John joined the baseball team as well as the football team. At first, he was on the Junior Varsity Team. He quickly rose to the Varsity team with his deft skill.

John was fast! He could run, throw, and hit - all thanks to his father's early training. John's father, despite his Chief of Police duties, always made time after school to faithfully continue to practice the art of baseball with his son.

During John's freshman year in High School, the Chief brought him to have a tryout at the Tri-County and Twilight League. John and another boy, Kenny Gregory, were the youngest there. In this league, the players were average age twenty-eight. They let John and Kenny Gregory, his good friend, play because they did not have enough players in the league. Despite such a vast age difference, John played just as well as players over ten years his senior. John and Kenny played with the Tri-County League evenings, Saturdays, and Sundays until he went to college. Many scouts watched the games.

Out of high school, Kenny got drafted to the Detroit Tigers minor league affiliate. However, John wanted to attend college rather than play professional baseball as he was only eighteen at the time.

John applied to study at the University of Tampa and he was offered a half scholarship to play baseball there. The University of Tampa was a small college, but an athletic director from Bridgewater High School, Joe Vaccaro, encouraged John to attend the University of Tampa.

Just like high school, in addition to baseball, John also excelled at football. At the University of Tampa, John played football for only three weeks. He walked off the field because he decided that he just didn't want to play football anymore; baseball was his sport of choice. John told his football coach, Coach Turner, that he had a better chance of making it to the pros playing baseball.

In Tampa, when John walked onto the baseball field, the coach knew that he could run, but it had been a while since he had been at bat. He hadn't swung a bat in two months, but John was kept on the team because he was fast; he had a good arm and could throw the ball.

John recalls that when he looked at the "cut" list, he was surprised that his name was not on it. John was given the position of right field on opening day for the University of Tampa Spartans team.

John had a twenty-seven-game hitting streak, and he was leading the nation in hitting, at the time. Out of all the baseball teams in the nation, John came in second or third in the nation and then he made second team all American.

Every day there were scouts present at the game, an average of ten per game. John's skill did not go unnoticed. After John's third year in college, scouts came after him right and left from Atlanta up to the Yankees. At this time John was 20 years old - old enough to leave college should that be his choice and move up to the majors. However, John decided to remain at the University of Tampa and finish his degree.

John was considered a prospect for the Major Leagues. Ultimately, John got drafted by the San Francisco Giants who picked John ahead of other teams. He was selected by the

San Francisco Giants during the third round, as the fifty-sixth overall selection, of the 1976 amateur draft, as a centerfielder. While at Cedar Rapids "Sly" (his baseball nickname) was the outstanding player on the team where he played alongside future major league player and manager Bob Brenley, among others. In 1976 as an outfielder, John was part of the Pioneer League All-Star Team.

Sadly, a major league career was not in the cards for John. He sustained a shoulder injury in 1978. At that time, "Tommy John" shoulder surgery[1] was virtually unheard of. John's injury to his right shoulder prevented him from throwing in the outfield and doing everything else a baseball player was supposed to do. Thus, John's quest for the Major Leagues abruptly ended. John eventually returned to South Bound Brook to start a new life, his baseball career over.

In 2016, John was inducted into the Bound Brook High School Hall of Fame for athletic achievement. Anyone who wishes to visit the halls of Bound Brook High School can see his photo plaque adorning the hallway by the gym.

If you search the internet, you can find all of John's baseball statistics during his brief career. However, be sure to search John, not Johnny, Sylvester. In 1926, a little boy named Johnny Sylvester was kicked in the head by a horse resulting in life-threatening complications. Johnny Sylvester was a huge fan of Babe Ruth, aka "The Babe". While little Johnny was in

[1] Editor's Note: As noted on the Johns Hopkins Medicine website, "Tommy John Surgery, more formally known as ulnar collateral ligament (UCL) reconstruction, is used to repair a torn ulnar collateral ligament inside the elbow." Named after the first baseball pitcher to undergo the procedure, Tommy John Surgery allows the athlete to return to the sport roughly six to nine months following the procedure (on average). https://www.hopkinsmedicine.org/health/treatment-tests-and-therapies/ tommy-john-surgery-ulnar-collateral-ligament-reconstruction

the hospital, Babe Ruth paid him a surprise visit. "The Babe" also signed a baseball for Johnny, which said that he would "knock a homer" for him. Babe Ruth did exactly that on the promised game day.

Johnny Sylvester passed away in 1990. However, John Sylvester lives on.

John frequently visits South Bound Brook's local mini-mart where he enjoys chatting with the locals. If you ask John about his baseball career, his face will light up. He loves to reminisce and regale tales of his baseball career to anyone who asks.

Apara's Story

I met John around 2009 at the – now long gone – Jimmy's Deli (formerly Vans). We got married in 2012 and were married for almost ten years.

Unlike John, I had zero athletic ability. I was the kid picked last in gym class. The kids used to moan and groan when I got "stuck" on their team. I couldn't run, hit, or kick a ball to save my life. Then, ironically, I got married to a former athlete. Thanks to watching the 1986 Mets with my dear grandfather, I had acquired a fair amount of baseball knowledge to understand whenever John spoke about his baseball playing days.

Forty-five-plus years later, John's baseball card still occasionally appears on online marketplaces. However, they don't last long because when I see his cards for sale online, I collect and buy them whenever I see them.

Lastly, referring back to the Babe Ruth/Johnny Sylvester story, John has a cat aptly named Babe Ruth Sylvester!

R.I.P. John Anthony Sylvester
9/2/54 - 9/15/25

Editor's note: We thank Apara for sharing this story with us and our readers. John passed away days before this book went to print. We are privileged to include John Sylvester's story in our anthology.

Looking for
Shad(enfreude)
Bill Hemmig
with illustrations by
Matt Lydon

This is the story of this story.

I've lived within a fifteen-minute drive of Lambertville, NJ for the past three decades, nine of them in the city itself, and although it's changed a lot and continues to do so, I'm still happy to call it home. A thriving manufacturing center in the nineteenth century due to its location along the Delaware River, the Delaware and Raritan Canal, and a freight railroad line, Lambertville declined with the ascendance of highways and trucking. Both canal and railroad ceased to carry freight, and the value of the city's Victorian housing plummeted. Then, in the late 1970s, as low-cost housing will do, it began to attract young artists, who in turn attracted gallery owners, antiques dealers, restauranteurs, and others looking for a quiet place to settle and a Victorian house to restore. Today the city has its thriving Victorian mojo back, minus the factories. Houses are beautifully maintained, the former railroad station is a restaurant, and the old canal towpath, where mules once pulled the canal barges upriver, is a state park, complete with native plants, waterfowl, and glimpses into the back gardens of the Victorian homes along the path.

I decided to set a story in Lambertville.

There are three events that I consider the high points of Lambertville's year. Halloween, for one, has over the past decade gone completely over the top, especially on North Union Street, where a local art teacher, now retired, populates her front porch and yard with a crowd of life-sized handmade ghouls that out-Tim-Burton Tim Burton, arranged to hint at sinister stories, and most everyone else tries bravely to match her. People come from miles around to take in the gruesome sights.

Sparkle Week is a longstanding phenomenon that happens in late April. For one week, city residents are allowed to drag to the sidewalk everything they'd like to get rid of—regardless of number or size—and the city will have it all hauled away. Mountains of discarded furniture, barely used exercise equipment, tools, books, toys, you name it. In reality, of course, Sparkle Week is an enormous city-wide yard sale where all the items are free. The residents prowl the streets adopting their neighbors' trash, the result being that year after year, if you're a regular, you'll recognize the same objects in different pickup locations. People also come from miles around for this.

I suspect it's no coincidence that Sparkle Week occurs immediately after the Shad Festival. Shad Fest began in 1981, just as Lambertville was starting to awaken from its postindustrial slump. Specifically, it was billed as a celebration of the return of the shad to the Delaware, which began two decades earlier after a huge cleanup effort downriver once again made the river hospitable to shad migration.

At any other time the shad is a saltwater fish, but when the urge to breed takes hold it suddenly, salmon-like, prefers fresh water and heads upriver, where local residents have since the 1880s been waiting to "haul" crowds of them in. Remember the Cole Porter song in which

the singer demands to be served shad roe?—*that* shad. Mostly, though, Shad Fest is a huge carnival, "two-days, filled with hand-crafted art, jewelry, home goods, a variety of delectable food, music, and fun for the whole family!" as described by the local Chamber of Commerce, which now organizes it. It, too, attracts folks from miles around.

I hadn't attended Shad Fest in years, not since the late nineties; introvert that I am, I can take only so much of crowds and festivals. That year there were a few stalls where one could dine on shad, and the smell—I don't know if I smelled the fish or the roe but the aroma was more than somewhat off-putting, and I love fish.

I devised a plan. Shad Fest 2024 was fast approaching and, without an idea for a short story in my head, I would go there, a notebook in my pocket, eavesdrop on revelers, and write down interesting things they say. I would then compile all these quotations into a narrative that would express the spirit of the celebration. I texted a friend who lives in Philadelphia. I'll call him Gatsby, which is the name he uses socially (a story for another time). He's much more outgoing than I am, so I figured if I spent the festival weekend with him at my side we'd have a more adventurous time and I'd collect far more interesting snippets of dialogue.

He phoned me: "What the fuck is a Shad Festival?"

I set out to explain it. It took him a while to comprehend the life cycle of the shad and then, when I got to the festival itself, I lost him completely.

"That sounds horrible!"

I then played the I-need-your-superior-skills-at-chatting-people-up card and he agreed to come up, for my sake.

I managed to secure what I think was the last somewhat reasonably priced hotel vacancy for miles—in New Hope, just across the river in Pennsylvania, for Friday evening into Sunday morning, figuring that we might as well have the whole experience (plus Gats trashes my place whenever he comes for a weekend and I'd prefer he trash a hotel room).

Friday arrived, and I stopped to pick up some wine on my way to check in at the Lodge when my phone went off outside the store (dialogue approximated):

"I'm really sick. I can't go up there."

"What's wrong?"

"I don't know but it's bad. I thought it might be COVID but maybe it's spring allergies hitting me hard. This is ridiculous. I was a landscaper my whole adult life and nothing. I want to cut my own head off. I have to get something for this."

"I have to spend the night at the Lodge by myself?"

"You're a grown-up. Go nuts."

"Well, get something and come up tomorrow."

"I don't know. Sorry, man."

"Get better and call me in the morning."

The cabin turned out to be a one-bedroom apartment with a full kitchen and a cavernous living room with minimal furniture randomly placed. I unpacked and then, armed with my blank notebook, made my way to the old Presbyterian church in Lambertville, the social hall of which provides a venue for the Shad Fest Poster Art Display and Auction. Each year, regional artists and hobbyists are asked to create an original poster commemorating the year's festival, and hundreds of them are displayed in the hall on Friday evening as a preview, some for a silent auction that collects bids all weekend, and some for a live auction on Sunday afternoon. Proceeds fund two $10,000 scholarships awarded to local students pursuing a college degree in the fine, performing, or culinary arts. The scholarships are named for Jim Hamilton (1931-2018), one of Lambertville's biggest personalities in a city of many outsized personalities. Scenic and interior designer, architect, chef, restaurateur, Hamilton helped create the Shad Fest in 1981, as a testimony to Lambertville's resurgence. His design and entrepreneurial achievements include the funky-elegant-eclectic Swan Bar (theme: American history), the Boat House (all things nautical, packed into a charming two-story saloon), and his restaurant, Hamilton's Grill Room (rooms like stage sets featuring enormous reproductions of famous nineteenth-century French paintings). He was a tireless fundraiser, once organizing a thousand-guest alfresco dinner in the middle of Union Street to benefit the fire department.

Inside the entrance to the social hall, Carol, a friend who's active in the local arts scene, was staffing the table where visitors could pick up a photocopied catalog and register for the live auction. She introduced me to an elderly gentleman who told me about one of the posters, entitled *Shadenfreude*, (get it? Shad-en-freude—from *Schadenfreude*, a German term for deriving pleasure from the misfortune of others) and insisted that there's a line about "Shadenfreude" in Beethoven's *Ode to Joy*.

"Freude, schöner Götterfunken," I hummed silently. And Beethoven didn't write the text, but never mind. I recorded the remark in my notebook, delighted that it boded well for gathering a great collection of quotes. I never did spot

Shadenfreude as I made the rounds of the displays, but no doubt it was fabulous and not a fiction on the part of the old man. The posters available for the silent auction, the majority, were at one end of the space, and the ones reserved for the live auction, by the professional artists who command the best prices, at the other. I met Charlie Groth, a colleague at the college where I work and a long-time Lambertvillian, who was cruising the displays with a couple friends. I mentioned that I hadn't been to the Shad Fest in a long time because of my lack of comfort with circus atmospheres, and she remarked that the poster preview evening is different because the artists and other attendees are here to raise money to further the success of young local artists, and to commemorate the importance of the shad to Lambertville. Saturday's and Sunday's circus has less to do with shad, she concluded, and more to do with the arts and the community.

I toured the posters. There were, of course, countless depictions of shad, some by artists who had clearly never seen one: witty graphics (three shad in top hats and pumps engaged in a Rockettes kick line; a 1930s starlet playing chess with a bright green, leering shad); fanciful renderings of shad in their habitat (three semi-abstract shad à la Paul Klee; a pretty purple flounder-like creature entitled *Poisson d'Avril*); tributes to Lambertville and its people (a giant yellow shad gazing quizzically down at tiny people on the canal towpath; a poster dedicated to a local woman who was on the US Olympic swim or diving team, with a shad in a red, white, and blue swimming singlet leaping out of an 800-meters-deep pool); and semi-vulgar near-puns ("Oops! I Shad My Pants!").

There were also numerous still lifes, including one with a

lone tin of shad or shad roe on a white tablecloth, but some with no fish references at all; complete abstractions that could have resembled views from underwater; and the questionably relevant (a realistic lion licking his chops—did he just consume a shad?).

At the center of it all, the Shad Queen held court. The Shad Queen is a local merchant who's worn the Shad Queen crown for years. She wore a wild patchwork gown of shad- and river-related fabrics—shades of blue and green—including a hood festooned with exotic fishing lures and topped with a hand-painted shad sculpted to scale (pun 

intended; it's easy to get caught up in the fishy atmosphere).

For the length of my visit I tried to overhear conversations and inconspicuously record snippets in my notebook. Eventually the Shad Queen took to the podium, thanked everyone who'd had a hand in the preview, and announced various judges' awards to thunderous applause. I snuck out, returned to the cabin, and enjoyed a couple cocktails at the neighboring bar before calling it a night, still wishing Gatsby had been with me (for the reactions of an outsider if nothing else; his would have made the best quotations—well, maybe tomorrow), and still wishing I'd located *Shadenfreude*.

Saturday morning I had breakfast at a nearby pub and planned my day, Gats or no Gats: I would wander the Shad Fest collecting overheard dialog, have lunch at some point, and then at 1:00 head for Lewis Island, where there was to be a shad hauling demonstration. I got a call from Gatsby announcing that he was feeling better ("It had to be damn allergies!") and would take the train up from Philly and where would I be. I told him my plan and he said he'd get himself to the Lodge and I should leave the key to the cabin with the office clerk.

I parked my car in a pay lot in New Hope and walked across the bridge to Lambertville—best to avoid attempting to park, or even drive, in Lambertville on Shad Fest weekend. The weather was perfect and the Fest was predictably hopping. Vendor booths lined the first few blocks on North Union Street and spilled into cross streets. A rock band was performing at the far end of a small, repurposed parking lot. A man on stilts dressed as the carnival attraction he was wanded enormous soap bubbles into the crowds, to the delight of children. A food and beverage court occupied the former bank parking lot at Union and Bridge, and a Beer Garden was set up in the parking lot of Lambertville Station, the old railway station. I was amused to discover that a major sponsor of the festival was Lambertville's recently established and ultra-hip cannabis dispensary.

My desire to overhear conversations led me to get close to the vendor booths which somehow led me to over-shop, even though I don't often enjoy shopping. I bought an official Shad Fest '24 T-shirt. I bought a bottle of herb-and-black-pepper-infused artisan olive oil. I bought another T-shirt, this one hand-dyed with a forest theme. I bought a bracelet of blue tiger's eye beads.

Eventually I looked at what I'd recorded in my notebook

and saw to my dismay that things had gone straight downhill after *Shadenfreude*:

"Would anyone like a flower?"

"I'd think that might be difficult for you."

"It's a beautiful day for the Shad Fest."

"But I didn't go in it yet."

"Let me know if there's anything I can help you with."

"Choose the wand that speaks to you." This last was collected from a woman selling handsome hand-carved and decorated wooden Harry-Potter-like wands. I asked her to tell me which wand was speaking to me, and she said that only I could make that determination. (There's a gem shop upriver in Frenchtown and whenever I walk in the staff has no problem pointing out which stones are speaking to me; thus the purchase of the tiger's eye bracelet, as I am apparently in regular need of tiger's eye properties.) I then questioned my need for a wand, magic or otherwise, thanked her and moved on.

Gatsby texted me that he'd arrived at the Lodge and was happily stashed away in the cabin. It was already lunchtime and my story of overheard dialog had no discernible arc, wit, or appeal. Despondent, I toured the food trucks and finding little of interest, and long lines at what may have been of interest, and 1:00 fast approaching, I headed toward Lewis Island and the shad hauling demonstration, thinking to myself in a near-panic that there had better be a truckload of zany eccentrics at this thing, chatting their heads off.

When I reached the bottom of Coryell Street, where a path leads to the footbridge connecting the mainland to Lewis Island, I was perplexed to see no mob amassing for the demonstration, only a handful of people on the island and another scattered between me and the footbridge. The gate on the mainland end of the footbridge was closed and Charlie Groth was standing at the bottom of the path. "You came back!" she said when she saw me.

I said that I'd come to see the hauling demo, to which she responded that the demonstration was cancelled: there'd been a lot of rain recently and the river was too high for a haul, plus at this height the currents made the wooden footbridge hazardous for a crowd. I probably groaned audibly. The zany eccentrics I counted on were still back on Union Street saying utterly innocuous, unzany things.

I explained my plight to Charlie, which led to chatting about the festival. She expanded on her comment at the poster preview, observing that the Shad Fest celebrants are mostly unaware of anything beyond the Union Street carnival midway. So it was a shame that the hauling demo had to be cancelled because it's the only opportunity to educate visitors about Lewis Island and its shad hauling traditions. The Lewis family's been hauling shad since the 1880s, and Bill Lewis, Sr. established the Lewis Island Fishery in 1918. It was Bill who managed, after much campaigning, to obtain government help in the 1950s to correct the river's environment. (Charlie is a folklorist as well as a member of the hauling crew, and studied the Lewis family and their shad hauling traditions from inside for many years, and published a book on the subject.)

The complete term is *haul seine fishing*. In short, a net, the length of which is determined by the condition of the river and is no more than ten feet deep, is stretched between a boat and the western shore of the island, with members of the crew at both ends. Slowly, both ends of the net are pulled downriver. By the time the southern point of the island is reached, the two ends of the net have been joined and the catch is brought on shore. If the river is too high for the net to touch bottom, there's no point to the haul because the fish will swim under it.

Even then, educating the public is an uphill climb: people assume the demo is a historical reenactment when in fact it's business as usual in a hauling season that's more than two months long; many miss the backstory of how the Lewis family led the formidable charge to get the Delaware cleaned up, which led to the shad's return; sometimes the crowd would actually boo if the haul brought in empty nets.

"But sometimes," she said, "they do get it." And she proceeded to relate to me the hauling demo of Shad Fest 2004.

Fred Lewis, Bill's son and head of the fishery since 1961, passed away in the middle of the hauling season and days before the Shad Festival. Fred had a big, generous personality and was a revered figure in the Lambertville community, leading the fishery to thrive just as his father's successful efforts to get the river cleaned up were showing incremental increases in the shad population.

His funeral fell on the Saturday of the festival. Members of the crew served as pallbearers. After the funeral, the crew changed into their hauling clothes, with the addition of black armbands. This haul would be a memorial. It was a good day for a haul and when the festival throng arrived for the demonstration, expecting a good show, they were met by the armbands and by flowers from the funeral set by the entrance to the crew's cabin, which quieted them a bit. Charlie herself explained to them why this would be a very special haul, what Fred meant to his family, the fishery, and to Lambertville, what the family accomplished, how the fishery will endure. The crowd became hushed. This wasn't a reenactment, a performance, an entertainment. Everyone on Lewis Island at that moment was a participant in the heart of the Shad Festival. My mind, too, became hushed.

One of Charlie's daughters appeared, and I excused myself. Ravenous at that point, and still with no material, I headed back into the crowd. At Lambertville House, a handsome stone hotel on Bridge Street that traces its history back to 1812 (still there as I write this), I somehow managed to get a table on the front porch in the middle of everything. I ordered a seafood salad and a vodka martini and watched the crowds, sulking. Shortly thereafter the hostess started telling walk-ups that she'd be able to seat them but there would be a twenty-minute wait before anyone could take their orders because the kitchen was backed up. I blessed my timing. I ordered a second martini. I watched the revelers. How completely foreign this was to the story I'd just heard.

Charlie's words came back. Fred Lewis's memorial haul, which I now felt that I'd actually attended, had grounded me. It came to me that I had my story: *this* story, the story of the story, the story of the shad and the festival and what they mean to this place. I texted Gatsby to say that I'd meet him at the cabin after walking off the martinis. With a satisfying sense of closure, I didn't return on Sunday, packed up my notebook, skipped the poster auction, and Gats never did see any of the Shad Festival.

I felt bad for him. I enjoyed the feeling. I guess I found my Shadenfreude.

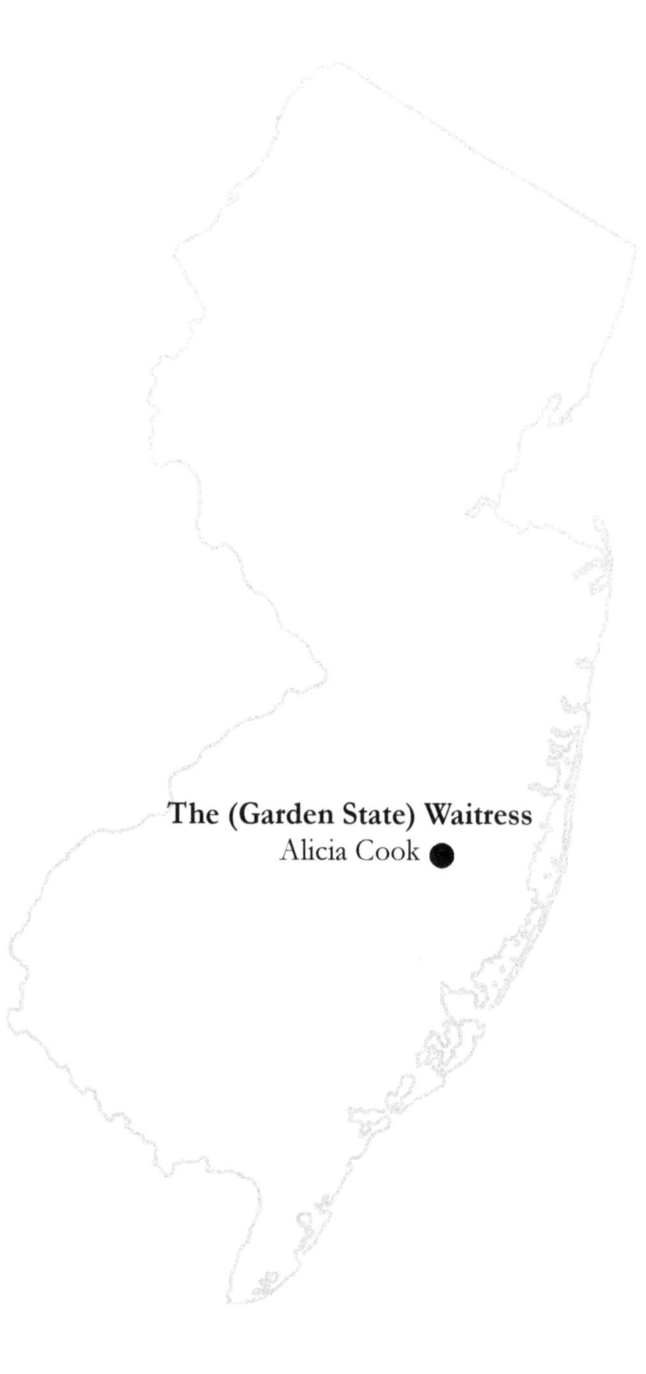

The (Garden State) Waitress
Alicia Cook

The bell above the door never stops dinging. Orders shout through the kitchen window like bullets—*short stack, side of bacon, rye toast, taylorhameggandcheese*. The coffee flows. The linoleum floor sticks. The oversized, crudely laminated menus shine. And Denise smiles.

She smiles for the regulars who know her name and for the bennies who don't. Her name tag reads *Denny*, because no one calls her Denise anymore. Not even her daughter.

It's just after 10 a.m. on a Saturday, the second morning rush in full swing. Denise swears she feels her phone vibrating in her apron. But it's a phantom buzz; just her nerves, maybe the rattle of a forgotten fork in her pocket, maybe nothing. She presses her hand to her body anyway, hoping.

Nothing.

The diner demands more than it gives. Her section's full, her feet hurt, and the last time she lost track of her kid was on a Saturday shift just like this; she was slumped in a bathroom stall at Wawa, barely breathing.

The eggs Benedict at Table Nine needs hollandaise. The man at the counter wants decaf and is still paranoid about the drones. Somewhere behind the order pad and syrup pumps, her heart beats like a rabbit in a snare.

Marie was supposed to come home last night. Denise boiled macaroni and set the table for two, a dumb little thing she does every time her teenage daughter spins lies about coming home. She kept the gravy on low till midnight, before calling the hospitals and jails she had saved in her phone.

So, yeah, this isn't an abnormal Saturday for Denise. Marie was barely seventeen the first time she didn't come home. There'd been rumors, and then needles, and then ambulance lights. Now, NARCAN sat next to the sinus spray in Denise's medicine cabinet.

"Denny, Table Five needs a refill," someone calls. Denise nods, automatically, a ghost in compression socks.

She fantasizes, sometimes, of slamming every plate to the floor and screaming that her baby is missing again. That she might be dead. Or worse. (Yes, there are some things worse than death.) The way she's expected to survive the possibility of outliving her child and still fold napkins into triangles is starting to really get to her.

But no one wants to hear all that from Denise. They want ketchup. They want their hashbrowns crispy. Even in places where almost everyone knows your name, you're still invisible when it counts.

Finally, her phone rings. Racing to the walk-in cooler, Denise answers, "Marie?"

"What?" the slurred voice says—alive, high, and annoyed. "You called me like ten times. I'm fine."

"I didn't know that."

"I'm fine."

"You could've—" Denise's voice catches.

There's a pause, enough time for Denise to picture her daughter's head nodding, then: "Mom. Seriously. You worry too much."

"I'm your mother," Denise whispers. "That's what mothers do."

"I'm fine. I gotta go. I'll call later."

Click.

Outside, Table Nine still needs hollandaise.

Jimmie Leeds is
a Terrible Friend
S. Atzeni

****

Galloway Township

It was a deer. Clearly. Born into the family Cervidae, cursed to wander this Earth as a swift-footed ungulate, sustaining itself on herbaceous delicacies homegrown in the Garden State. I was absolutely certain it was a deer, but this was my fifth house call and I was exhausted. I didn't want to have it out with an eighty-year-old woman in front of her home, who was now crawling through her garden bed looking for anything that resembled the gates of hell.

"It was just here a few days ago," she muttered with the same ferocity as someone who has misplaced their keys.

"Well, ma'am," I began, the words rolling off by rote, "oftentimes, a demonic portal has a strict statute of limitations…"

The woman straightened herself and glared at me. "I saw what I saw." She gestured to my notebook, turned to a completely empty page. "Why aren't you writing anything down for your little magazine?"

That "little" magazine is one of the most well known paranormal magazines in the country. Off-center Garden State investigates the best of the best in the ghost-hunting pantheon: ghouls, zombies, hotel poltergeists, hellhounds, murderous hitchhiking spirits, and, of course, the Jersey Devil. Granted, with the last one, everyone claims to have a close, personal friendship with the one and only Jimmie Leeds. Yet no one can ever seem to locate him when I'm standing on their property, ready to interview.

Either Jimmie Leeds is a terrible friend or our callers were liars.

Right now my blank page was mocking the woman in front of me. "You don't believe me, do you?" she said accusingly, glaring at me from her oversized garden hat.

"I do, ma'am," I began in what I hoped was more professional than frustrated. "And I recognize that Mr. Leeds may be playing a joke by not appearing…"

"You think I called you because Jimmie Leeds was in front of my house?" she said. "I called you because the Jersey Devil was here."

"Aren't they the same thing?" I asked.

The woman gaped at me as if I told her that Wawa Hoagiefest was cancelled. She narrowed her eyes at me, considering what was standing before her. "Let's start over," she said. "Come inside and I'll give you the full story." When she saw my hesitation, she added, "I have snacks."

Like any hero worthy of Joseph Campbell, I crossed the threshold with the promise of baked goods and freshly made iced tea. And just like the heroes before me, there will be no snacks, only suffering.

Inside, the house had that cluttered-but-cozy feeling. Meaning, I wasn't fearing for my life that a pile of newspapers from the Reagan era would fall on me, but I also wasn't counting on a place to sit. "Come through," she said, gesturing to a dimly lit room. Upon seeing my hesitation, she added brightly, "I won't murder you, my dear."

"Thanks," I said. I didn't believe a word of it, but Miss Manners would agree that reassuring someone that they won't be murdered as they moved deeper into your slightly-cluttered, poorly-lit home was a polite gesture. Once inside the living room, I was met with a mix of differently patterned furniture, a small paddleboard, a sword on the mantle, and three dead plants. Please note my omission of the word "potted," for these plants were propped dead in the corner of the room, sans pottedness, as a mix of rotted roots, dirt clumps, and brown leaves.

Following my gaze to the plants, the woman said simply, "They know what they did." She briskly cleared off a stack of faded quilts from a chair, ready to get started. I sat down - a bit too forcefully - forlornly looking at the coffee table covered with dusty magazines and broken car parts, knowing this table had not been cleaned in years and therefore would not be producing any snacks.

The woman perched on the arm of a couch where she could stare directly at me. "I called you here because I saw the Jersey Devil." She glanced pointedly at my empty notebook page.

"Oh! Right," I said, lifting my pen to the page. I was hungry, tired, and the chair was lumpy. "First, let me get your full name, please."

She narrowed her eyes. "Why do you need that?"

I blinked. "To quote you?"

She shook her head. "No chance. Don't quote me. Just say 'anonymous source.'"

"Wait, you don't want credit for seeing the Jersey Devil?" I asked.

"Why would I want credit?"

Because this is what we do. I thought to myself. We "investigate" and you get your fifteen minutes of fame. Aloud I said, "So people know who you are."

"Why would I want people to know who I am?" The

woman furrowed her brow. "Maybe I can reschedule with someone who has more experience."

"Ma'am," I said evenly. "I can assure you that I have the experience to properly report a Jersey Devil sighting. If you don't want your name in the article, then I won't include it. Now, can you tell me your story?"

"My story?" The woman stood up. "What does my story have to do with this?" She left abruptly, but I could still hear her voice. "I want to talk about the Jersey Devil, not myself." She came back to the room with a bag of rolls. "Here," she tossed them at me. "I promised snacks."

I held the bag of misshapen rolls to my chest. They were stale. "Thanks," I said.

"So, the Jersey Devil," she started again. This time she didn't sit back down. She began pacing around the room, kicking away household items that got in her path. "He took something from me and I am trying to get it back."

"Wait, wait," I said, scrambling to get my pen and notebook in order. The stale pile of carbohydrates rolled off my lap and into a sad lump at my feet, competing with the plants in the corner. The rolls know what they did.

Seeing me finally take interest in her story, the woman smiled triumphantly. "Yes, he took something from me. So I've been hunting him ever since."

"And this isn't Jimmie Leeds?" I asked.

"No, the Leeds family has nothing to do with this," her tone was reaching high levels of exasperation. "But that cloven bastard made a powerful enemy when he messed with me."

"Maybe we can start at the beginning?" I asked meekly.

The clutter, the plants, the sad rolls, and this convoluted conversation was making my head spin.

"Finally!" the woman threw her hands into the air. "That is the most sensible thing you've said all day."

Spoiler: she didn't see the Jersey Devil. No one ever sees the Jersey Devil. After hours upon hours of questions, tangential conversation, and arguing, it was concluded that the Jersey Devil did not mess with this woman; rather it was a family of long-tailed weasels (born into the family Musteldae) that had caused a ruckus, thus leading my subject to develop a long-standing feud with the Jersey Devil. Upon discovering her mistake, she doubled down on the hoof prints outside which, it turned out, was a deer. Clearly. Born into the family Cervidae.

As with most of my interviewees, she wanted company and someone to validate her experience. I left her home with a scribbled-over notepad, a dead plant, and stale rolls.

****

Ewing

"Alright, let's take five, everyone!" shouted the almost-director. I say "almost" because they were scrambling to complete the film in order to get enough credits to graduate and because they kept wandering off to eat from crafty. Crafty consisted of their mother's banana bread, six bottles of blue Gatorade, two egg and cheeses from the morning, and stale rolls, which were mysteriously placed there by an unknown person. The film shoot became a race against time - finish the scene before we lose daylight or before the debilitating stomach cramps brought on by foods that didn't belong together took hold. Guess which option won. Go on, guess.

Since we had so much downtime, I took the opportunity to walk around the set. I was hired as script supervisor (being paid in coffee gift cards, which is a step up from stale rolls) on the short film *The Lady in White*. It was supposed to take place at the actual tree in Newark, where the devastated forever-bride met her tragic end, but the film crew couldn't get the permits in time, so we were filming in the woods behind the college. When I arrived, the director exclaimed brightly, "It looks like Newark enough!" It did not. But a creepy wooded area with a creepy tree in New Jersey can be universally creepy if you just believe in yourself.

"Look at these footprints!" exclaimed one of the crew members. "I bet it's the Jersey Devil!"

Immediately, all heads swiveled in my direction. They were waiting for an expert opinion. Oh right - that's me.

"Um, probably not," I said slowly, trying to hedge the disappointment that will inevitably cloud their faces. "We're in Central Jersey and the Jersey Devil likes to stay close to the Pine Barrens."

"But it's, like, not unheard of, right?" ventured another guess.

"Well, no," I said. "But it's pretty rare. Also, this would be The Lady in White's domain."

"Not really," scoffed another. "We're not really in Newark."

I don't know if my $15 coffee gift card balance was worth it. Luckily, the director came back, rather timidly and still bent at the waist, to take their seat. We were called to our places.

"Let's have a conversation with our expert," the director/screenwriter/Lead suggested. The director, producer/craft services/Old Woman #2 (again, the director's mother), assistant/Bystander #1 (director's little brother), and cinematographer/costume supervisor/Legal/Bystander #10 (director's roommate) gathered around me. "Can you share a bit about The Lady in White mythos please?"

"The mythos?" I repeated. "Um, sure. So, the tree is haunted by her ghost and we can tell she's been there by the white X on the front."

"But what's her purpose for being there?" asked the cinematographer/costume supervisor/Legal/Bystander #10.

"Well, I don't think she wanted to crash into that tree," I said.

There was a chill in the air. "Wait, what?" the director/screenwriter/Lead said. "What do you mean 'crash?'"

"It was a car accident," I said. "On her wedding night."

The director/screenwriter/Lead groaned. "I didn't know that."

"You didn't know how she became The Lady in White?" I asked.

The group around me shook their heads. "We thought she lived in the tree," said the assistant/Bystander #1

****

Titusville

Things I have learned while scouting Gravity Hill:

1. Like most strange- and maybe true - stories in New Jersey, this one is built from tragedy.

2. The tragedy is usually buried under the urban legend

of it all, turning it into a weird moment of sideshow that gets posted to forums and social media.

3. Gravity Hill isn't as creepy as some of the stories - in fact, it's sweet to think that the spirits are trying to protect you.

4. It's horrible to think that in your attempt to be a part of this story, you make the spirits think you need protecting and aren't just someone whose car is in neutral, waiting for spectral guidance. It's a form of hubris that can only come from the living.

5. Trust your driver. Some people think it's funny to pretend the car breaks down or stalls, leaving everyone in the car to panic - believing the spirits can turn malevolent if we wait too long.

6. It's illegal to attempt Gravity Hill. Like, SUPER illegal.

7. Rolling backwards in neutral and picking up speed, praying that maybe a spirit will step in, with a driver who thinks it's funny to pretend the car stalled, is not my idea of a good time.

****

Berkeley/Lacey border

"See anything?" my managing editor asked me. The service wasn't great and my phone kept cutting out.

"Not yet," I answered, leaves crunching under my feet. "It's so creepy here."

"Well, they don't call it 'Double Trouble' for nothing," my managing editor said. "Let me know if you can spot any remnants of UFOs. Oh, and get quotes!"

Tyler, age 16, who will not answer why he's in Double Trouble Park on a weekday afternoon: "Nah, I didn't see any UFOs. Except that time when I almost did. But it was a car. So almost?"

Debra, age none-of-my-businnes-why-do-you-need-that?, who is out trying out a new birding hobby. After the divorce, she's trying to get out there, but it's really hard, you know? So maybe this bird thing will work out. Also: "It isn't UFOs you're looking for - it's a meteor crash."

Mr. Whitmore, age 78, who is out walking his very small terrier that has decided it hates me and wants to rip me apart: "Meteor crash? I don't think so. I mean, the trees are really flat and it looks very suspicious, but I was always told it was just a tornado from long ago. I think I saw Jimmie Leeds around here a few months ago - you should really check on that instead of this nonsense."

Oliver, Tyler's friend, age 17, who is also doing "nothing" at Double Trouble: "It's definitely UFOs. I mean, come on, that's why they're covering it up. It wasn't aliens, they would just say so. But they don't, so it's definitely aliens."

Matt, Tyler and Oliver's friend, age 16, who is taking a walk to find himself in nature and nothing else: "You know, I saw this documentary once about aliens that tried to take over Earth. They had to plant a virus into the ship."

They? You mean Jeff Goldblum?

Matt, age 16, still not getting it: "Who? Yeah, I guess, he's like some army general or something? Anyway, he planted the virus in the alien spaceship and it made the aliens allergic to water."

I think that's two different movies.

Tyler, age 17, who may be the smartest one of the group: "Dude, the water one wasn't a documentary about aliens. It's about baseball."

Thank you for your time, gentlemen.

Debra, the expert bird watcher who looks good for her age: "Look, I know it seems weird, especially the Cedar Creek black hole that sucks up your phone battery, but it's just a bunch of flattened trees. Nothing fancy. Hey, is that a Wilson's bird-of-paradise?"

It is not. I believe it's a blue jay.

Debra, expert bird watcher: "I saw a documentary about these genetically engineered blue jays that can mimic people."

I think that's *The Hunger Games*, not a documentary.

Debra, who definitely gets it: "Ha! Not yet it isn't."

Mr. Whitmore, age 78, whose tiny little dog definitely wants to eat me: "Those kids are up to something in these woods. I see it all the time. Their imaginations and Lord knows what else gets in the way of common sense. The world is obsessed with aliens. Hey, remember that movie with Will Smith?"

Independence Day, yes. Great movie.

Mr. Whitmore, age 78, who is now wrestling the horrid, rabid creature into the car. "Now that's how you take down extraterrestrials! You should put *that* in your magazine."

****

Bayonne

Wednesdays are usually weirder, I thought to myself, absentmindedly spinning in my chair. I glanced at the other desks around me, watching my colleagues type up their final articles, call last-minute sources, or secretly watch videos on their phones. It was a quiet day.

A few more minutes ticked by before my editor walked out of her office. "Look alive, people, we got another call," she announced. That's what she does - she never *says* or *speaks* or *points out*; she *announces* everything. As if we're a real life newsroom and getting an exclusive with the Watchung witches will get us that Pulitzer.

"Another call about what?" I asked. I'm excited for the interruption, but I moved slowly like a cat caught in a sunspot. I suddenly felt very sleepy.

"It's another Jimmie Leeds sighting," my editor announced (again). "This time at the Wawa on Route 37."

"What is he doing there?" someone asked.

"No idea." Another announcement. "But let's get someone out there. This could be it."

"What could be it?" I asked. "We'll finally get a Jersey Devil sighting?"

My editor, about to make another proclamation, paused. "Do you think we're going to see the Jersey Devil?" She said it slowly with a bit of concern.

By now, all of my colleagues were looking at me with concern on their faces. I felt my face flush. "Um, yes?" I answered. "Isn't that what we do here?"

A few people chuckled before getting back to work. My editor considered me. "My office, please," she turned toward the door.

Now my face was as heated as the Gates of Hell (just pick one, it doesn't matter). I followed her into the office, sure I'm about to be fired.

She gestured for me to sit down and I did, taking in the beautiful New York City skyline from the windows. She followed my gaze. "It's funny, isn't it?" she said. The announcer's tone is gone and it's replaced with a hushed one filled with reverence. "No matter how many times I look out this window, I'm impressed. To think how close the City is to us." I didn't need to ask to know that "the City" is a proper noun. Everyone in Hudson County learns this before they can form their first sentences. "The City" is New York City and it's right there to gaze upon.

"It is something," I said.

"But," she began again, "I also feel like it's a consolation prize. 'Sorry you aren't us, but you can look at us.' I know New York and New Jersey are neighbors, yet sometimes I can't shake that we're the little sibling always trying to imitate the older one."

I nodded, not quite sure where this is going. She continued: "The City is fascinating and interesting and something to behold. It has history and amazing people."

I nodded again. "Definitely."

My editor shrugged. "Maybe. But New Jersey is also fascinating, interesting, and something to behold. We also have history and amazing people. And -" she paused dramatically. "We have a Jersey Devil."

"Okay…"

"Look, I know how your last few weeks have been. I've read the reports. And you think these stories didn't bear any fruit. However, the stories are still there. When you head out into the field, you aren't looking for the weird or strange or off-beat. You're making a connection to all of the stories that make up New Jersey."

I stared back at my editor, who was extremely calm in this moment, leaning toward me and fixing me with a steady gaze. "So it all matters?"

My editor smiled. "Yes, every story, every quote. It's all part of what we do here."

We let those words hang in the air. "Make these stories count," she said. "It's all part of this mysterious, beautiful, weird state."

I stared back at her, afraid to nod again in case I looked like a broken bobblehead. I stood up to go.

"Good luck," she said to me. "Make sure you get some good quotes."

"From Jimmie?" I joked.

She snorted. "If he's willing to go on the record."

I gathered my things from my desk and prepared to go. It

was going to be a bit of a drive, but the promise of a Wawa helped. Maybe I'll stop by the Judy Blume rest stop on the way. I waved goodbye to everyone else in the bullpen and walked outside. The waterfront air hit me with its complicated breeze - refreshing yet with a stale olfactory note. I'm never sure what the smell is here, but it's been engrained in my senses for as long as I can remember.

Normally I look out toward the water for one last look at the City before I head further into New Jersey. Today, I didn't feel a need to. Instead, I squared my shoulders and headed toward my car, the City at my back and the Garden State ahead of me. Jimmie Leeds or not, I was going to get my story.

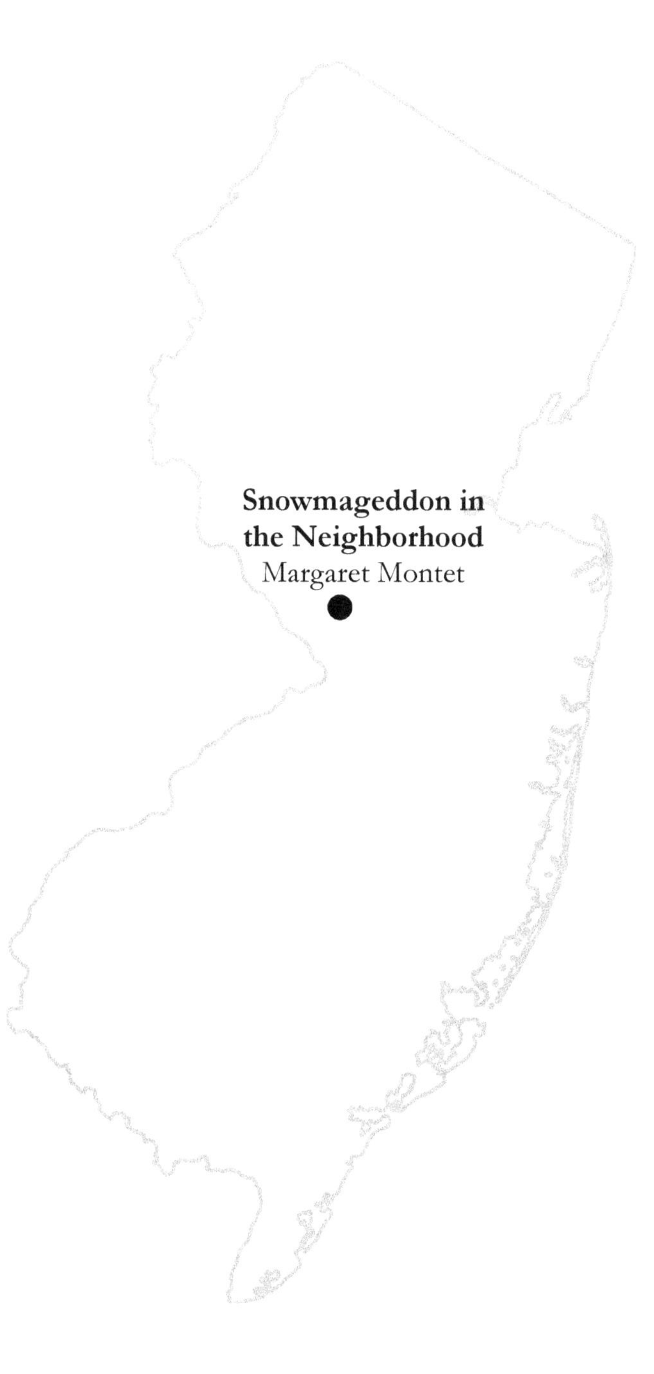
Snowmageddon in
the Neighborhood
Margaret Montet

I flew to Paris to meet a friend from Ohio, and on the plane I read Agatha Christie's Miss Marple stories. Specifically, I was reading those from *The Thirteen Problems* (1932), a collection of short stories each told by a different character. They bring their quirks, experiences, and knowledge to Miss Marple's house on Tuesdays and challenge her to solve the mystery in each story. This is a common device, creating an amalgamation of characters with varied personalities from which mayhem or drama ensues. Agatha Christie, Ann Patchett (in *Bel Canto*), *Murder, She Wrote* and *Gilligan's Island* on TV, and the 1962 film, *Exterminating Angel* (Luis Buñuel) which is also an opera by Thomas Adès all feature this literary template. In each of these examples, a group of people is thrown together and interacts.

Agatha Christie's group, The Tuesday Night Club, is not in any danger while the members of the group tell stories with curious solutions. I was inspired. I'm a travel writer, so I imagined a group of neighbors telling travel mishap stories instead, and during a blizzard. The biggest storm I have experienced in my family's Jersey Shore house was dubbed "Snowmageddon" by the media. Let's use that! I imagined neighbors coming together at a central house (mine) during a snowstorm to alleviate the boredom, anxiety, or whatever they are feeling during Mother Nature's tantrum. My house sits on a corner where five streets meet. It's kind of like Paris's Étoile, but without an Arc de Triomphe in the middle.

This is autofiction: the stories of travel mishaps all happened to me, and the blizzard happened to this location with me in it in 2010. The stories here will be assigned to various characters based on real neighbors, dead and alive. I thought it would be fun to get them all in the same room. You, the reader, won't necessarily know where the line is between truth and fiction.

To get the ball rolling, I told the story of my recent trip to France. I could have taken my story in many directions, but I started by explaining the limits of my French. "I was able to communicate mostly in French," I said, "although my skills consist mostly of nouns with some present-tense verbs, and a few pronouns." It's true: my confidence with the language has developed. I was thrilled that the French people with whom I interacted were able to understand my French. It felt like a new level of competence actually being understood by native speakers.

"I wish I could leave it at that," I said, "that this trip showed my French improving. My actual takeaway is something else. I was broke, busted, and financially embarrassed. How did this happen? My particular credit card was accepted only at hotels, train stations, and some taxis. I had some leftover euros from a previous trip, but I was not able to extract any cash from an ATM because of a constellation of issues. First, my bank claimed that they could not unlock my card for use at French ATMs as they always had before. Their suggestion was to stand at an ATM, attempt a withdrawal, let it fail, and then a text would come through from the bank asking if that was really me. If I answered in the affirmative, a new transaction would be possible. ARE YOU KIDDING? No, they weren't, so I hoped an ATM situation would present itself where I could play that waiting game without appearing as an Ugly American or inconveniencing any native French people or tourists. That was my hope.

"It wasn't to be. My other obstacle was my phone. I signed up for an international plan as I have done in the past, but I could not activate it abroad because I was without the required toggle switch. I could be standing at an ATM in the dark, in the rain, for hours waiting for a text that would never come! While enjoying free Wifi in the hotel, I texted boyfriend Fred at home with descriptions of the two problems, and he attempted to tackle them the next day.

"The bank was a dead-end since he is not on the account. The phone people were more helpful, especially when he told them I had gotten nowhere with their international helpline. That tech showed Fred I'd have to reset something and demonstrated on his own phone, same as mine, and they sent me screen shots of the steps I was to take. This worked and I would now be able to GPS walking directions for sightseeing, but I never did get any euros.

"This, unfortunately, is what I'll remember from the trip. I had to rely on my friend Jessica to buy food, souvenirs, and other incidentals that weren't attached to a hotel. I wasn't exactly a freeloader since I prepaid the hotels and bought the Bayeux train tickets, but I felt like a needy, inexperienced traveler nonetheless. By the time I go to Spain in the spring, I'll have a new travel-friendly bank and a few back-up credit cards! In time, I'll be able to spin this story to showcase my ability to work around barriers without getting upset, and my good fortune to have great friends!"

THE SINK

My neighbor Kate came by. She saw the candlelight from the jar candle I lit on the centrally-located dining room table when the power went out. She came by to keep me company. She was delighted to see that there was already a group of neighbors assembled. Kate has always been a good neighbor, and as a nurse is a font of useful information. Although she eventually switched to the local hospital and was present when I was born, she had started out at the Coast Guard dispensary and always addressed my parents as "Montet." Her husband Cyril died many years ago, and ever since she has tooled around wearing his old clothes with her white hair in pin curls, held against her head with black bobby pins. We rarely see her in her white nurse's uniform. She never wears scrubs. In summer, Kate frequently stops by at breakfast time to chat, bringing her own cold beer and refusing eggs and pancakes.

"We're sharing travel mishap stories, Kate. Do you have any?" She accepted a cold brewski from the makeshift snow fridge on the porch, and regaled us with this:

"About a decade ago, I set out alone for a nurses' conference in Camden (about ninety minutes north). This was when I was driving our Studebaker, and I was worried about the voltage regulator. I had shown Cyril how we would have to tap it periodically so that the battery would not go dead. This involves reaching down inside the engine compartment which is inconvenient when one is wearing a white nurse's uniform.

"I rarely leave this county, so this trip was a big deal. I always felt it was my responsibility to stay abreast of the latest nursing techniques, so off I went. The voltage regulator would not be the problem, but the tire blowout was! I had a spare, but no jack to fix it. It was late in the day, so no service stations had anyone to help. I had to leave the car on the side of the road and walk to a nearby motel carrying my valise and nurse's bag. I was relieved to get a room with a phone in it, so I called my brother. He could bring a jack over to change the tire in two days. I called the conference organizer and arranged to have a ride from the hotel to the conference the next day.

"For a few moments, I thought all of my problems were solved, but then I remembered that I hadn't packed enough clothes and skivvies for the unexpected extra day. I began washing things in the sink when all of a sudden I heard a creaking noise and the sink basin fell into the vanity. I turned the water off immediately and wondered what to do next. Could I brush my teeth the next morning in the shower? Probably, but I decided it would be best to report the issue right away."

"We have no plumber on-site to fix it," the desk clerk said. "The only other vacant room we have is on the other side of the property. We're almost full because of a children's soccer tournament."

Kate continued: "So I walked to the office to get the new room key, then back to the old room to get my valise, nurse's bag, and now a few articles of dripping wet clothing. I had to make two trips. It was then that I realized that the motel was adjacent to a large adult entertainment complex and truck stop. Truckers were standing around in silhouette smoking. I could clearly see the orange dots from the lit ends of their cigarettes and cigars."

"Oh my gosh, Kate! Did they bother you? Were they loud?" Georgette had never been in a situation like that!

"No, no," Kate said. "In fact, the few that I met when I went over for supper and a beer were very kind. Wearing Cyril's clothing I blended in. That's why I usually wear his clothing now."

The assembled guests loved Kate's story and her telling of it. Kate seemed bewildered by the giggles occurring, to her, at strange points in the story.

BOOM!

As the blizzard went on, we would hear loud booms. We couldn't imagine that people were out there driving around, but if they were they probably slammed into each other, or crashed into telephone poles or trees. The booms made the house shake a little as a nearby auto crash might. The side roads appeared impassable and we didn't see any vehicles on the main road except for a plow and the occasional utility truck not restoring our power. What was going on out there?

The next day when the snow tapered off, I would figure out what was causing the booms. Tree branches were falling everywhere. This region at the southernmost point of New Jersey features many Eastern Red cedar trees (Junipers) and other trees more common in the southern states. These trees, especially Junipers, have flat leaves that catch the snow. In that Snowmageddon storm, we ultimately got two feet of snow instead of the usual one or two inches. It was too heavy for the leaves and branches. They fell. Big branches fell. For weeks after the storm the sounds of chainsaws and wood chippers could be heard from dawn to dusk. The aroma of diesel exhaust was strong throughout the neighborhood.

I was sad that my dad's prized Southern Magnolia lost some branches for the same reason: big flat leaves caught the heavy snow. The Magnolia survived, but many red cedars succumbed. When the tree service trucks and guys with chainsaws finally finished, it looked like the neighborhood had gotten a too-short haircut.

Magnolia wood is not good for much, but according to my tree identification book, red cedar wood repels moths and is used to line hope chests and closets, and to make souvenirs with seashore town names painted on. I wonder if any of my neighbors thought of selling their red cedar wood!

REFRESHMENTS

We took a break from our story-sharing for some warm beverages and snacks. I showed the gang the cool LED light Fred had given me. It was about the size of a playing card and an inch and a half deep. It had a hook on one end that I could hang on my shirt to illuminate the stove and counter as I worked.

In order to use the stove, I turned a gas burner on and held the flame of a long-handled lighter next to the ring until the burner was lit. This is how I boiled water for tea, cocoa, and oatmeal, and I had prepared a complicated soup, Zuppa Osso Bucco, earlier that day with my light and lighter. I had purchased the many ingredients including ground veal, vegetables, white wine, and lemons, before the storm hit.

Around the table and its centrally-located jar candle, we sipped our beverages, ate coffee cake, and some sampled the soup I had made earlier. We got to talking about other snowstorms in our seashore town. Few rivaled this one, though.

CLIFF WALK

Claire and her next-door neighbor, Marian, were my

mom's friends. They live down the street, and their houses face the houses between Georgette and Calvin and Gladys and Gene. Claire is the traveler, while Marian usually stays home to keep an eye on things. Both had adventures to share.

Claire told us a story about stopping off in Newport, Rhode Island, to see the Gilded Age mansions on her way to visit her son's family in Maine. "I stayed in a quaint inn which was too quaint for me. It was like a bedroom in a house with only a lock in the doorknob. There was no reception desk in the lobby, or deadbolt, or emergency panic button. One afternoon, after a day of sightseeing, I came "home" to find a man standing on the stairs, focused on me. I had to pass him to get to my quaint bedroom, and although I was nervous, I went for it. As I shot up the stairs past him, he said, 'Hey, aren't you the Door Dasher?' That's why he was eyeing the little brown bag I was holding with my breakfast pastry in it!

"The inn and the mansions are not my main story, though. I became intrigued by the Cliff Walk. This is an innocent-looking sidewalk past the massive rear lawns of the famous mansions."

"The Marble House and Breakers? We saw those," Georgette interrupted.

"Yes, those are two of many that are open to tourists," Claire said. "My guidebook described this walk as a unique perspective on Newport with ocean waves crashing on the boulders at the foot of the cliff on one side and the mansion lawns (and Salve Regina University which used to be a private mansion) on the other side. The sidewalk of the Cliff Walk was generally even with the mansion lawns, but the ocean and its boulders sat at the bottom of the cliff. I decided to take a stroll. The brochure advised walkers to enter at Narragansett Street where the walk is easy, but the further north you go, the tougher the terrain becomes. I wasn't worried—I walk all the time. I wanted to walk far enough to see the backyard of Edith Wharton's former Newport home, Land's End.

"I entered the Cliff Walk where suggested. The waves breaking on the boulders below created a photogenic scene. I could imagine the posh Gilded Age lawn parties happening to my right, and then there was one! Salve Regina University was having a graduation celebration on their lawn.

"The smooth sidewalk gave way to gravel, and I thought this must be what the brochure meant by rougher terrain. You couldn't push a stroller on this part of the path, nor was it ADA compliant. I kept walking, and as the gravel rocks changed from pea-sized to kiwi-sized and then apple-sized, I noticed there were fewer families and older folks on the trail. The people hiking near me were wearing hiking boots and had really long legs. I was wearing cute Sketchers sneakers and my legs are short. I kept going because I really wanted to see Edith Wharton's house, and the walk was exhilarating.

"Soon the gravel turned into boulders the size of VW Beetles, and each had to be climbed over to progress. Was Edith Wharton's house worth it? Would the trail go back to fine gravel? No and no.

"I finally had to admit that these VW boulders were more than I could manage. If I broke a bone or sprained an ankle, how would I be rescued? An ambulance would not be able to navigate this terrain. Would I be air-lifted by the U.S. Coast Guard? This would be embarrassing and expensive, so I turned back. I made it to my car and began the next leg of my trip.

"Weeks later, while looking at the maps and tourist literature I had accumulated, I realized I could have seen the front of Edith Wharton's house from the main drag, Belleview Avenue.

"I'm so glad I didn't break a leg."

MADRID

Gladys and Gene from the yellow house were next to tell a story. They had taken a trip to Spain almost two decades ago and had practiced the language for months ahead of the trip. *Donde esta la biblioteca? Una mesa por dos por favor!* They learned that no amount of memorized phrases would cover every situation. "I'll admit Gene was better at grammar and full sentences," Gladys said, "but I may have had a larger vocabulary at that time. Now I just remember some nouns.

"We had spent some time in Madrid, roaming around the three big museums (*museos*) there and touring the palace. Every day we had breakfast (*desayuno*) in the hotel restaurant, and I fell in love with the fresh-squeezed orange (*naranja*) juice made with Valencia oranges. We had a great time in Madrid, but it was time on the fifth day to take the train to our next destination, Granada. There we would see the magnificent Alhambra and the Generalife gardens.

"First, it was necessary to navigate the Atocha train station, purchase the proper tickets, and get on the correct train. We also had to get some sort of breakfast since we had skipped *desayuno* at the hotel in order to get to the train station bright and early."

Gene took over the story here. "This was my first time

abroad relying on my Spanish. I was nervous, trying to speak in complete sentences and remembering to say *por favor* and *gracias*. The ticket agent had no English at all, but I was able to communicate what we were after by pointing at the word 'Granada' and the time on the timetable. He was able to enter the required personal information from our passports. Gracias!"

Gladys put down her cocoa for the next part of the story so that she could use her hands for emphasis. "The train station was beautiful with gardens illuminated by skylights. There were even frogs and turtles in those leafy gardens! We went over to a small casual restaurant that had posters hung up of the food they had available. I told Gene that I would like a chocolate donut, an orange juice, and an *agua*. I'd sit at this high table with the suitcases while he ordered. He could point at the posters when necessary to communicate our selections. He went up to the counter and spoke to the clerk. A cafeteria-style tray appeared and was soon populated by my donut on a small plate, a bottle of water, a coffee and breakfast sandwich for Gene, and a pair of sandals in a cellophane bag. Sandals? My Spanish isn't good, but I could do better than that! Why do they even have sandals here?

"It was a mystery. After my orange juice was added to the tray, Gene returned to the table where I sat. He laughed at my confusion about the sandals and pointed to one of the food posters."

Gene: "There was a special deal that day. If you bought a breakfast sandwich, orange juice, and coffee, you got a free pair of sandals. Between us, we had the required items and so we earned the sandals. I still wear them, although not in blizzards."

ESPRESSO

Mrs. Heckins has lived diagonally across the Étoile for decades, and before I was born she and her son and daughter would come to our house to play Canasta (a card game) with my mother and sister. With both husbands away, my dad on a U.S. Coast Guard ship and Mr. Heckins working in Philadelphia, this was welcome socialization for all involved. Until the Cape May-Lewes Ferry opened in the 1960s and Cape May tourism gained momentum in the 1970s, the southern tip of New Jersey was remote, especially in seasons other than summer. Television existed, but reception was terrible and there were only three possible channels anyway. There was no fast food, but there were luncheonettes.

Mrs. Heckins played the organ at the little neighborhood church, and her son, once grown, preached there. Because of this commitment every Sunday and her quirky personality, I didn't think she ever traveled. She seemed amused by our stories, and to my surprise she shared one of her own.

"I don't know if you know this about me, but I detest coffee. I hate the taste of it and the aroma! My story is that I went to South Philadelphia with my cousin to pick up some sheet music that belonged to a retiring choir director. I didn't know the man, my cousin did, and this was a windfall for our little church. I'd better be on my best behavior.

"All went well at first. The choir director was already convinced that he should donate the music to us, so I just had to appear grateful, and I was! Then his wife invited us to be seated at a small table. She came out of the kitchen carrying a lovely old hostess tray with a plate of cookies and…espresso! Before I knew what was happening, a tiny cup and saucer were placed in front of me. I did not want to be rude or ungrateful and lose my chance at that music, so I endeavored to take tiny sips alternating with bites of cookie until the espresso level in my cup went down. I felt like I had consumed gallons of the heinous stuff, but the level of brown liquid in the cup did not seem to be going down! I drank and drank tiny sips, gradually becoming queasy. Finally at the halfway mark I stopped, and my cousin and I left with three big boxes of music. I was queasy for the rest of the day. I felt so ill and tired when I got home two hours later that I didn't even open the boxes to inspect the treasure."

Kate the nurse said, "I think you might be allergic to coffee. That is how my stomach behaves when I accidentally eat shellfish."

"What do you mean 'accidentally?' Can't you just avoid it knowing you're allergic?" This question came from the far end of the couch.

Kate replied: "I do avoid it, but sometimes people cook with it and don't warn you. Since we live by the ocean, crustaceans are everywhere. Some people think they are delicacies. I don't. Why would you put lobster in perfectly good macaroni and cheese? I'm like Heckins—I don't want to be rude. I'll be queasy for days from one tiny shrimp.

MOBY

The refreshments were consumed and we looked around the room to see who hadn't shared a story yet. "Georgette and Calvin, you're up!"

Georgette and Calvin lived next door and had two dogs about the size of mine. They are the friendliest neighbors ever, and we chat often. Our dogs have playdates. They used to take a lot of trips in their enormous RV, and I could see Georgette on one of the armchairs, itching to tell their story. I wondered where this story would take us, so I asked her:

"Massachusetts! Specifically the Berkshires. I wanted to see the writer Edith Wharton's home there. It's called the Mount and it's the home she had built after she got tired of the Gilded Age life of Newport and New York. The estate features lawns, gardens, and woods, and anyone can show up with a picnic basket and dine alfresco. The lunch restaurant on the porch had just opened for the season, so we ate there

"While in this area, we discovered that there is a museum in a house where Herman Melville wrote *Moby Dick*! He would sit at a table in front of a window and stare at a large, gray, rounded-top mountain in the distance and pretend that it was the whale. The idea brought smiles to our faces. Our tour ended after seeing his writing spot and we were invited to hike the field and forest around the house called Arrowhead."

"Isn't it strange that each place we visited there has a nature trail of some sort?" asked Calvin.

"It was nice to have an opportunity each day to stretch our legs and breathe the fresh mountain air," Georgette agreed. "We walked around the perimeter of the field and then through the woods and back to the parking lot. We were, by the way, in our car for this trip and staying in a clean, quiet, modest hotel on the highway. After our day of touring Melville's place, it was a relief to lounge on the crisp white sheets of the bed and look at the books we bought there. I was enjoying a short book called *I and My Chimney* about Melville and the fat stone chimney at the center of his house.

"Suddenly, 'Oh, no!' I saw a tick embedded in my calf. I could have picked that up at any of our destinations, but I'm guessing it was from Arrowhead. That bug needed to come out of my leg now, but I had nothing to remove it with… except…embroidery scissors. I did my best amateur surgery and got the tick out. Of course I described the adventure on social media, making it clear that it came from Melville's house, Arrowhead. 'Moby Tick!' a friend commented.

JOEL AND MARIE

"My story is backwards," Marian said. The 'mishap' *part* happens before the travel part. The travel part, actually parts, went smoothly and were delightful.

"It all started when I was reading my personal email one day at work when there wasn't much happening. I came across a very personal email, in French, from a guy named Joel to a gal named Marie. He was telling her about his recent trip to Paris and how he was sorry to have missed her. I got the gist of the message, but I didn't understand the slang. *Prendre un pot*, despite what you may think, means to have a drink.

"I felt bad for the guy, Joel, knowing that his message didn't reach Marie, so I carefully crafted an email to him, in French, explaining that his email came to me in error. I figured out later what had happened: Marie and I have the same last name (Robert), and the same first initial (M) and our emails are very similar: MRobert@yahoo.com except, hers requires an FR after the Yahoo like this: MRobert@YahooFR.com. Joel had forgotten the FR.

"Joel and I began a fun electronic correspondence after that. When I found out he was a barrister in London I suggested we write in English. When he found out I hadn't read *The DaVinci Code* yet (it wasn't in paperback in the U.S. yet) he begged for my address and sent me a British copy.

"The following spring, Joel announced that he was coming to New York City for work. Would I fancy meeting for brunch? Indeed, I would! So I took the train to Manhattan and walked to the Upper West Side restaurant he suggested. We had a delightful brunch, he with a Bloody Mary and me, the teetotaler, with orange juice. Then we went our separate ways.

"The story doesn't end there! Facilitated by Joel, I also began a correspondence with Marie. Her English was better than my French, so we wrote in English. She was a lawyer in Paris. Eventually, I told her of my plans to visit Paris to present a paper at the American University there. She suggested we meet for dinner one evening. When the day came, she met my friend Sue and me at our hotel near the École Militaire and showed us how to use the Metro (the subway) to get to the Tuileries. We ate at a lovely café there surrounded by twinkly lights, and I asked her how to pronounce a few challenging words for me: I remember *chantilly* (whipped cream) and *grenouille* (frog). I had chantilly on my crepes, but no one ate frogs' legs!

"Sue said she felt like we were in a movie. It was magical. Marie escorted us back to our hotel via the Metro, and Sue and I talked about that evening for a long time.

THE BAY

We chuckled over Marian's story and how it could be a movie plot. Everyone was getting nervous about the snow piling up outside, but no one wanted to actually go out and see what it looked like. We used our imaginations instead.

"I bet the bay is frozen today. Last time I was able to log on to Facebook, I saw that the ferry was cancelling a number of crossings to Delaware because there's too much ice."

"Remember that one year they got the Coast Guard ice cutter to break up the ice so the ferry could cross? Were you living here then?"

"One of my favorite things to do is to walk up to the bay beach after it has been below freezing and see if the little breakers are frozen. The bay doesn't get big waves like the ocean—those wouldn't freeze—but sometimes these little waves freeze as they break onto the shore. It's not worth taking a camera, though. In a still photo you can't tell that they are frozen!"

Two days after the storm, after enough snow had been shoveled and the side streets had been plowed, a group of us with dogs walked down to the bay to see what we could see. Most of the houses were vacant as part-time residents stayed in their regular homes in Philadelphia, Central and North Jersey, New York, and wherever. We knew from robocalls to our landlines that power had been shut off in the neighborhood because there were so many wires down. They were everywhere, it seemed, and we did our best to keep ourselves and our dogs away from them.

Finally, we made it to the bay four blocks away. We saw a sight none of us had seen before. Two feet of snow, drifted deeper in some spots, sat on top of the dunes and the beach entrance. No one shoveled the beach show! None of us could see over the dunes and we certainly couldn't navigate the trail to the beach in snow up to our thighs. We'd have to skip the frozen waves this time.

Spending those long hours of storm and no power was easier with friends. We supported each other and made it through the challenging time. The power came back on after four days of decreasing indoor temperatures, but the deep snow lingered longer. We still reminisce about the fun we had during Snowmageddon, and we still share stories of travel mishaps!

Life in the Garden State

There are only a handful of 24 hour diners left in New Jersey, but having spent the better part of my twenties traversing the state in the quietest hours of the night, I have a genuine appreciation for anywhere I can get pancakes, eggs, and bacon at two in the morning.

~The Unforgiving Loop (*Writing on the Walls*)

North Jersey diners get the most attention but as someone who has driven all over central and south Jersey, I love getting an omelette and coffee at the Ewing Diner. Chrome exterior, plenty of booths and tables, it feels like a diner that could be from 1955 or 2025..

~Scott Napolitano (*How The Story Ends*)

While it's no longer here, Mastoris Diner in Bordentown was truly a place of wonder. It was a labyrinth of mismatched dining areas and, for all the times I visited, I never sat in the same room twice. They also had a menu the length of the OED, and each meal seemed to be cooked with the intention of feeding a small family.

~Adam Wilson (*Order Up*)

Favorite Diner

Life in the Garden State

In the pandemic, Adam and I would drive all over New Jersey with our two-year-old sleeping in his carseat. The world was so quiet and as we drove, it gave us a chance to be present as a family. 2020 was a tough year, but it's those moments of New Jersey's beauty, the comfortable silence of the car, and the happy toddler noises from the backseat that held me together during that time.

~S. Atzeni (*Jimmie Leeds is a Bad Friend*)

I live in Newark, NJ, and not a day goes by that I don't walk, run, or drive through Branch Brook Park. It's beautiful in every season—especially during cherry blossom time and fall foliage. And nothing compares to the park after a fresh snowfall.

~Alicia Cook (*The (Garden State) Waitress*)

What I call the *Jersey Pancake Trail* starts in Somers Point, and weaves through Strathmere, Ocean City, and Sea Isle. A truly great drive will include all of these, the Wildwoods, and conclude in Cape May! Uncle Bill's to the Mad Batter, you can't go wrong!

~ Matt Lydon (*Platinum Platypus*)

Best Scenic Drives

Menlo Monster

Erinn Salge

Aubrey was perusing the 5 for $15 underwear display when the text came through. Purple boyshorts with daring black lightning bolts, so punk, like the girls who wore arm warmers, pink briefs with a suggestive row of buttons up the front, and one virginal white lace thong that she would have to wash in the sink to keep her mother from seeing, the way she'd washed the underwear she'd nearly ruined when she first got her period back in freshman year, long after it seemed everyone else had.

Have you seen this?

The text read.

She recognized the photo immediately, because she had taken it herself, in her room.

Around her a buzzing seemed to set in, the strains of "American Boy" by Estelle, which wasn't on the radio nearly enough, falling into the background as blood rushed into her eardrums.

Where did you get this? Audrey typed, clacking, then slid the pink Motorola Razr shut with a thud, like shutting it hard enough would erase the photo, erase the reality that the picture she'd sent, her body with its 17-year-old newness, clothed only in the very same kind of cheap underwear she was pawing through right now. Like she'd been caught in the act. At the scene of the crime. An underwear pervert - if Lisa had that picture who knows how many other people had it too?

She swept the phone open with her thumb and paged through her contacts for Sean, even though she'd memorized and forgotten and re-memorized the number last month when they'd broken up.

Huddling in the fitting room, she hunched over her full

bags from Aerie, from Bebe, from Clinique. This was not the way her night was supposed to go.

Surprisingly, he picked up on the first ring.

"Hello?"

"Sean?"

"Yeah?"

"Who the fuck did you send that photo to?" she hissed, her grip on the phone loosening with flop sweat, the horrors of being known, of being seen, of being perceived by so many when all along she had only intended it for him, her golden boy.

"You told me you deleted it," Aubrey stammered.

"Need any help in there?" a chipper voice called out and Aubrey flashed her teeth at the clerk who backed away and pulled the curtain closed tightly.

Silence echoed through the receiver.

"Fuck," he said.

"Who did you send it to?"

"No one. No—just. Greg asked."

Greg, the shithead son of the local pastor whose youth group passed out promise rings at Valentine's and tiny fetal models to guilt you away from Planned Parenthood for your Mirena insertion.

"How did he know it even *existed*, though, Sean."

For a second she remembered his eyes on the day when he broke up with her for good, when he said they'd be friends, when he said it was better this way. Back to the way it was when he'd get her a Slurpee and it would mean nothing instead of everything, when they were all part of a big group of friends and before they became a satellite to that. His eyes had burned golden brown when he told her he'd delete the picture. Because they were *friends*. Because he was a *good guy*.

Which made her what, exactly?

"I'm sorry, Aubs," he said, and the nickname burned her again, the ease and familiarity of it.

"I didn't mean for it to get out."

If Lisa had sent it to her, maybe creepy Greg had only sent it to her. Maybe, maybe, maybe.

"It's kind of a big freaking deal," she said. "It's my body!" She strode out of the dressing room with her bags and a fistful of underwear that she paid for in a rush at the counter to the same bewildered salesperson who'd tried to help her. Monday would be school and only then would she know the real impact, how far the photo had traveled. When she'd taken it, her hands mashing her breasts together with the camera overhead, she felt sexier than ever before, some keeper of secret carnal knowledge unlocked on their fourth date together. But on the phone she looked like any other skank on Myspace.

***

When Monday morning came, two weekend days of sweating out who knew what, who saw what, who knew *her*, two things were immediately apparent.

Most of the school had seen her semi-naked.

And her debit card was missing.

Aubrey wasn't sure which was more upsetting or disorienting. All she wanted was a Frappuccino to face the day and she had one wrinkled dollar bill in her purse. As she walked through the double doors of Eagle Rock High School she saw a flicker in the eyes of Billy Carter, auxiliary friend, and immediately knew.

They'd seen it. So many of them had seen it. From the covered-mouth whispers of the brace-faced sophomores to the head nods from guys who'd never glanced her way before, she pulled down the two carefully-layered ribbed tanks she'd chosen as if she could cover herself in the past, go back, never take the picture.

She had to find Sean, and she had to—who knows. The rage she felt was electric, mixed headily with rage at herself for being that stupid, to think her friend deserved to see her, just because they were "dating." Like that movie where the girl sets her prom on fire. She stood in gym class picturing Sean's head bursting into flames, but even if that happened, well. The picture would still exist.

Lisa sidled up to her after AP Bio.

"Are you okay?" she said, anxiously, chewing the ends of her brown hair, a disgusting habit that Aubrey allowed due to loyalty.

"I'm fine," she lied.

"I'm sure not that many people saw it. And it's not like you're totally naked."

Mr. Britt, the Stat teacher walked by her and for a second a glimmer crossed his vision. Like he'd seen it, too. Aubrey shriveled inside.

"I just need to get through this week. Then APs. Then graduation. And I can fucking escape this town and these people and no one will know me at college."

"So, so true," Lisa affirmed.

"Can you come to the mall with me after school? I think I left my debit card there," Aubrey said. She wasn't sure why she needed emotional support to run this errand, but she had to believe the card was there or else the finely constructed shell of a life she'd put together would crumble, somehow.

She was called into the vice principal's office by the end of the day.

"It seems there's a photo of you circulating," Mrs. Tate, neck a deep crimson red, blurted out.

"That was private."

"Honey, you shouldn't be sending things like that. It could be considered child porn."

"Well, what about the person who actually sent it out?"

"We can't keep track of all that, dear," she said.

Aubrey felt the rage rising again, fire-in-the-blood, her pulse at her neck pounding as she gripped the armrests of the sad industrial chair.

"Well, maybe you should," Aubrey hissed.

"I hope this is a valuable learning experience for you," Mrs. Tate said, "One time I saw something on the Internet about how fast an image could spread. It was very powerful!"

Aubrey shook her head and laughed, the sound brittle and hollow, echoing out her pale throat.

"Am I in trouble?"

"We can't punish students for what they do in their free time. This is more of a woman-to-woman conversation," Mrs. Tate said.

"Well, is anyone going to talk to Sean about sending it? A more man-to-man conversation?" she pressed.

Mrs. Tate looked uncomfortable.

"We can't litigate every dispute between students."

Aubrey rose from the chair, hair on fire, and walked out of the office.

***

At the mall, the scent of the hot pretzels turned Aubrey's stomach. She felt like she might never eat again, but there was Lisa chomping away, the paper turned translucent under the power of the butter.

"When did you use it last?" Lisa pressed.

"I was at Charlotte Russe," Aubrey said, headed in that direction over the smooth, polished floor, her flip flops thwacking as she strode with purpose to the escalator.

In the store, the same salesperson stood at the register, petite nose stud twinkling under the warm lighting.

"Can I help you?" she asked.

"I think I left my debit card here. Friday?" Aubrey pressed.

"Name?"

"Aubrey Schlesinger," she said. The clerk punched in a code and the cash drawer opened with a thud. She pulled out a piece and located a small pile of colorful credit cards.

"Right here," she said, delicate french tips pulling the blue Wachovia bank card from the crop.

Aubrey exhaled, at least one thing in her fucked-up life fixed.

"Hey, are you okay?" the clerk asked. "You seemed really upset on Friday."

"Boy trouble," Lisa chimed in and Aubrey cut her a glare.

"Sounded more complicated than that."

At the risk of having another conversation about her tits with a random woman today, Aubrey took the card and headed towards the exit.

"You need to check out the last dressing room," the clerk called over her shoulder.

"The what?"

"The last dressing room. In the back. But not today. Let me check, hang on,"

The clerk opened a browser window and searched "Full Moon May 2008"

"Next Tuesday."

Aubrey scoffed, this weird Mall-witch telling her to come back on a full moon, like she understood.

"It's a special place," she said.

"Oh, like a coven meets here?" Aubrey said.

"Just come back. It will help. I can tell you need the help."

"C'mon, Lisa," Aubrey said. "Thanks for holding onto my card." She pulled Lisa by the arm out of the store and past the giant planters she had once been kicked out of the mall for sitting in as a pre-teen.

"What was that about?"

"Who fucking knows. Mall weirdo," Aubrey said, headed towards the exit and the last few weeks of shouldering a world where so many people had seen her boobs.

***

By the next Tuesday the situation had fluctuated from bad to worse. Sean not speaking to her, random guys from her class she never spoke to trying to touch her in the hallway, girls hissing "Skank" under their breath as she walked by. When she found out Jenn Untley was also going to Providence with her, dashing her hopes of escaping the situation fully, she cried in the last stall of the girls' locker room, bitter tears that slid down her cheeks and left her telescoping mascara pooled under her eyes.

She caught a flash of Sean leaving out the band hallway where he thought no one would see him.

"Sean!" she yelled out and he turned, a man caught by his executioner.

"What do you want?" he asked, and his response gutted her, a fishhook slid cleanly into her guts and turned them out onto the worn tile of the floor.

"Maybe a fucking apology for ruining my life?" she said, words that turned into sobs. Somehow, on some planet, her parents hadn't found out yet, but she was sure they would and the final nail would slide neatly into her coffin, sealing her promised senior summer shut.

"Don't be so dramatic, Aubrey, no one cares about you."

He turned and headed for his car and the familiar flicker danced in her belly where her guts once lived.

She headed for her car in the other parking lot.

She headed for the mall.

***

The same clerk was there, folding a T-shirt that read "Blonde But Bright" in lacy gold script, so impossibly flimsy the fabric shone through already, pre-washing and wearing.

"You're back," she said.

Aubrey nodded her assent, her freckled knees knocking. What was she doing here? Why had she come?

"It's a little early, but it should still work," the clerk said, leading her to the dressing rooms. A girl from school lingered near the chandelier earrings, her fingers brushing the beads without breaking eye contact with Aubrey.

"Just through here. Press hard," the clerk said.

Aubrey closed the curtain behind her again. The scuffed beige wall and tilted mirror, cleverly askew and leading the girls to believe they were taller, thinner, better, taunted her. Her raccoon eyes and tangled hair were a disaster. Her life was worse.

Aubrey pressed on the shared wall, then the mirror, leaving sweaty marks. Then she turned and saw the faint grubby outline of other handprints on the back wall and placed hers there. A chill ran down her warmed neck as she stood in one spot. *Bleeding Love*, remixed, played loudly as she just stood there waiting.

And then it came. That same fire, the one that had marked her for the past few weeks, made her wily and raw and red-hot to the touch, to the sight, coursed through her. Like it was coming from the wall but also meeting her somewhere in her belly. Her forearms edging out from her shrug sweater took on a reddish cast as her skin began to transform.

Scales, delicate reds and yellows and oranges, the colors of a firebird, of a fire bonding her, began to form over her arms. She felt an instant of pain as her tongue, the same one she'd kissed Sean's stupid face with, split at the end into a muscular, forked entity. But that was the only pain she felt. For as she became a monster what she mostly felt was relief. To be divorced from her human body, her human heart.

And also the comfort of knowing that there were other monstrous girls before her.

Somehow she knew she couldn't bare the mirror, so she remained with her back to it as the transformation proceeded.

The same clerk's voice rang out, the same chipper: "Everything okay in there?"

Aubrey laughed, a pleasingly deep rumble from the rib cage that now contained her terrible, monstrous heart. She ran her new tongue over her new teeth, the pointy tips a delightful prick to her senses.

"Take this," the girl called out, tossing an XL hoodie that read "California Dreamin'" across the chest. As Aubrey turned she caught a glimpse of her eyes, the irises a deeply unsettling, wolfish yellow. But there was something else in them that had been gone for weeks.

There was life.

She pulled the hoodie over her new body, delighted with her disappeared breasts, her smoothed out belly. She wished for a devil's tail but felt that was probably going too far. And where would she go next?

To Sean's.

Aubrey slid into her tiny Honda Civic, her new skin flashing out of the sleeves of the oversized hoodie. The sun had set while she was in the mall and she drove to his house by memory, back roads to the little neighborhood with the big houses.

But how to conceal her face, her new self, from him long enough to get close?'

The dark would enclose her if she could wait another half hour. She texted him.

I'm sorry for everything. Can we meet up and talk? Alone?

For as surely as the Gregs and Seans of the world closed ranks around one another, the promise of a female body could sometimes break that pact. She promised it once again, like she'd done in his car, like she'd done with the photo. She shed her clothes, her skin for him. And now she was new once more.

The Wendy's Drive-Thru lit up the night and as she sucked down a large fountain Dr. Pepper, cooling some of the fire the mall dressing room had imbued in her, she pondered her next move.

Sean's name flashed across the screen of her pink phone. She swallowed and slid it open.

Nah

That same deep, inhuman rumble echoed out of her. He didn't have time for her. But she had time for him.

She had all the time in the world.

Sean was taking shots on the basketball hoop outside his house when Aubrey pulled the car up and cut the lights. He was alone. Yes, he was totally alone. Even the porchlight was dark as the late spring shadows wrapped her up like one last gift to him. She had already given him so much.

"Sean?" she called out, deliberately throwing her voice into a delicate, more womanly, more *human* form. She did not know what she was, but she was no longer just a girl.

"Fuck," he muttered, and shot one last shot, a bad one that banked off and thudded into the soft, wooded area next to the house.

"Can we go for a walk?" Aubrey asked. Isn't that how it had started? In the woods, among the remainders of parties they weren't cool enough to be invited to mark the pine needles, empty beer cans and dead blunts that he'd sweep away for her to lay back. She glanced at her face in the mirror and knew that only her eyes had changed, that the scales on her arms and chest hadn't reached her cheeks or brow.

Sean rolled his eyes and shrugged. "What's there to talk about?"

"I wanted to apologize," she said, careful to avoid s-sounds that would reveal the parting of her tongue, the glorious change. The moon loomed high above them, round and full and maybe just a little bit red. Red like her.

"For what?" he asked.

"Making a big deal of things."

Isn't that why they'd broken up? Her emotions? Too sensitive, needs too much, too, too, *too*. Too everything.

"C'mon," she said, wishing she could unzip the unwieldy hoodie to show him some skin, except that she was no longer in possession of the same breasts he had once loved so much.

She slunk off into the woods and listened for his footsteps behind her. Sure enough, they came. Her ballet flats slipped among the dead leaves as she pulled the sleeves of the sweatshirt over her scaled hands. In a few steps, he caught up to her.

"Further," she said, leading him. Her third eyelid slid over her eyes for a second and she was innately aware of every other living, breathing thing in the woods with them. The owls, the bats, the clouds of mayflies she walked serenely through without swatting.

Finally they reached the clearing with the party detritus.

"Is there anything you want to say to me?" she said, still with her back to him. She cursed the moon for revealing her secrets as much as she wanted to thank it for giving her the gifts.

"No, I don't know why you brought me here," he said, a whine in his voice. His stupid, whiny voice. That he would take to UCLA next year and get new pictures of beautiful, naked, clueless girls like her. And send them along to new, even worse versions of creepy Greg. He didn't care. He wouldn't stop.

Unless she stopped him.

"Are you sure about that?" she asked. She turned slowly, feeling like her curls would turn into Medusa's snakes, feeling that her brand new acrylic tips would fall from her glorious curved talons, feeling like the fire she'd felt for the past two weeks would leap out of her throat and consume him.

"What the *FUCK??*" Sean called out. And then she knew for the first time that he was truly seeing her for the woman she had become. The rumble came from within her chest as she reached out and tackled him to the soft, spring-sodden earth. She reared her head back, incisors bared to the moon that made her, and sunk her teeth into his neck. The primal scream that echoed out of him gave her life, gave her power, made her somehow whole again. The taste of blood was honey on her lips, sweet and oozing. He pushed her off him and scrambled to his feet.

In his eyes was almost the same look as the first time he saw her naked, a fear and agony in it.

"Don't fuck with me, Sean Cartwright," Aubrey said, smearing the blood across her chapped lips. She fake-pounced and he whimper-screamed, turning on his heel. She pushed the sleeves of the sweatshirt up and saw her skin beginning to return to her pale peach hue, the scales receding under the fine blonde hairs she would shave during swim season.

Maybe it was better this way. To be a girl, vulnerable and talked about and hated and loved and loathed most of the time, with the power to drink blood when it really mattered. She owed that Charlotte Russe clerk a thank you. The blood wouldn't come out of the hoodie, though. She pulled it against herself, the chill of the evening settling in. She walked out of the woods and back to her car.

She headed to the mall.

Writing on the Wall
The Unforgiving Loop

There is an untrue narrative that graffiti is a sign of neglect. Many contemporary graffiti artists seek to redefine that narrative even so far as referring to it as "street art." Street art is a new form of public art that plays with traditional graffiti and tagging methods as a way to foster community, beautify neighborhoods, and rebuild a sense of civic pride.

This has been met with mixed results. At its best, street art can be a sign of a thriving community. At its worst, street art is a calling card of gentrification, where the same artwork that strives to reinvigorate invites attention from affluent individuals and high end businesses whose presence drives up the cost of living and in turn drive out the people who have called these places home. Keystone members of the community who have worked to maintain and rebuild their neighborhoods, even when others have forgotten them, are no longer able to afford the communities they fought so hard to save.

The photos in this series were taken across central New Jersey to document various communities' changing relationship with street art and the often-times blurred lines that can exist between a thriving community and an alienated one.

~The Unforgiving Loop

Street Art
Increases
Property Values

RISE UP

PAGX
DYZO
RUIN
BEBE
CITY KREW
PSYCHO
ZECER
ESA
KEST
GAK
GKILLA
WRB ROT
AFFIRMATIVE
YOUTH
KAEDE
REMANI
APEX
DJGUMBA
DREWONE
D10Z
KEL
AYB
TLWA
RIBS
GAK
REMAND
GUMBA
TCU33
DYZO
ARC
HER
SNAP
LOVE
X-CUL
SHEP
ONE
SAYS
DOES

Ophévie

Vulture

JC
JVC
58
E

Yeah...
I LIKE IT,
PICASSO!

FLEMINGTON

243

S.A.G.E.
Coalition
Crew
Excessive GENTRIFICATION DESTROYS THE BIODIVERSITY AND ECOSYSTEM OF A COMMUNITY"

LONG LIVE
NJ DIY

Selected Poems
Kathy Kremins

A Place of Many Shipwrecks

I lived every moment with the thought of your death
some imprint from my two-year-old self waving to you
from the sidewalk up to the window at Clara Maass Hospital,
holding mom's hand but reaching for you.
I spent childhood pulling you back to the world
of the living from your imagined death:
a massive heart attack while driving, and if
your weakened heart didn't kill you or us,
then smashing into a light pole on South Orange Ave.
S-curves surely would, or dying right in front of me
in mid-throw during our every night summer game of
catch and throw, or dropping dead at a funeral,
or a wedding, after another rendition of Danny Boy:

For you will bend and tell me that you love me, and
I shall sleep in peace until you come to me.

If only I could circle my island of fears but once.
Yet my heart like your heart is a fragile one, skipping beats
racing to catch what is just out of my reach.
How many cracks and healed scars can it stand?
Is it really stronger because of the losses, or is that what people say
to avoid the burden of missed beats, failed connections,
silent regrets, love undone, clogged arteries and veins, burst vessels?
So many things are fumbled out of life on an island of dread,
place of many shipwrecks and stranded dreams.

The Price of My Soul

-for Angela Davis & Bernadette Devlin

Tommy and Kevin jump us outside the library
knock the books out of Eric's hands into the snow
slap him and push him until he falls to his knees
cries for forgiveness for no reason, except his sweetness.
I back up two steps, place my three books gently
on the steps behind me safe from harm. The night
before, Bernadette Devlin commands my attention
points her finger directly at me, speaks fire
arm around Angela Davis, sisters shoulder to shoulder
declares a free and united Ireland in her/our lifetime
announces solidarity with the Black Panthers and liberation.
I rush those bullies, smash eyes, crack a nose, draw blood
splatters like spilled paint run down Eric's face
anointment to the hatred for gentle souls
my hands ball in fight, fear, and frustration
fists still clenched in defiance, devotion.

May Your Home Always Be Too Small to Hold Your Friends

-Irish Proverb

Before eminent domain destroyed my neighborhood, MLK and RFK were assassinated, the Vietnam War ended, Nixon resigned, my period began

> *all my uncles played cards once a month at the dining room table*
> *with JFK and Jesus keeping tabs on the game and every so often*
> *Uncle Jim (not my Dad's brother, Joe, or my Mom's brother, Mike)*
> *slept on our couch, always with his raggedy peacoat as a blanket*
> *and the Murphy kids surrounded the TV in the same living room*
> *with me holding the antenna, wildly cheering on the Miracle Mets*

Before AIDS, Aunt Mary drank herself into the Kate Macy Ladd Home for Women, Dad dead from a massive heart attack, Patty left me, Ken murdered, my hair turned grey

> *Dad finally owned a home at 62 years old, and with Barney the dog*
> *(whose given name was Baron but long forgotten) romping*
> *in the backyard with the Virgin Mary statue at the tree end*
> *and St. Francis at the other, peeking out from abundant roses*
> *my girlfriend kneeling with my father, four hands deep in the earth*
> *laughing with each other about something that I can't hear*
> *while Mom, Auntie Bride, and I set chairs in the garden sanctuary*
> *because church happened on these blessed Sunday afternoons*

Before Mom died a long death from Parkinson's-induced

dementia, Sarah and I divorced with the same love we married, I retired, medical neglect and sepsis killed Nick, Auntie aged away until her final breath, JMR slowly perished from demons and drugs, her kids lost to both of us in tragic ways, Hurricane Sandy, the happiest house sold, the bankruptcy, my years of wandering

The doors never locked because, over the years, keys were knocked
down air vents by the kitties (mostly Gerard, the crankiest cat) or
absentmindedly taken by friends who came and went in need of home,
thus, the sign posted in the entryway offering anyone who "broke in"
to take whatever they needed, but please, not the animals -
Calvin and Hobbes (bunnies), Twombley, Gerard and Marcel (cats)
Seamus (dog) and unlocked doors gave easy and early access
to the faculty and staff weekly gathering on the deck by the river branch
in the bamboo forest where we held each other in reverence, joy,
oftentimes productive disagreements and love. Always love. Always.

On Spectacles

I avoided them for years
despite a genetic predisposition.
The fact was, though, I wanted them.
Not as a fashion statement
or a fancy non-apparel accessory.
I wanted them so I could look smart
on those days when my math skills failed me.
But mostly, I wanted them for the days
when the school bully was on a rampage.
I knew my glasses would protect me.

You see, he lived down the street from me in a house
that became suddenly sad and dark three summers before.

I remember running with my neighbors toward the corner
toward the screeching, screams, and sirens.
I still see his mom rocking his little brother's broken body
as the frantic bus driver kept repeating through his cries,
God, I never saw him. God, I never saw him.
Yards away from the accident lay the boy's eyeglasses.
I imagined the bully would recognize I returned the pieces to
him
though it seemed as if his eyes went blind and his blood
drained out of his heart that August afternoon.

I didn't get glasses until I was 43.
And I had a bully in elementary school.

Half-Birthday

The full birthday I remember, vaguely
I was probably three, and my parents -
poor - (or maybe it was Aunt Bride
my guardian angel - living - who ran
Fireman's Insurance - well, she was
Secretary to the President
but you know what I mean) bought me
a miniature piano, beautiful blue wood
that I subsequently dismantled
since I knew how to unscrew and ratchet
from my Dad, who barely kept things running
but run they did as I did from my Mom's fury
knowing that even if it took me a day
to slow down and get caught, a spanking
was in my future, well, actually, a beating
though this poem needs soft touches
so I'm writing this on Arlo's half-birthday
five and a half is monumental, a tsunami
in a childhood of light breezes as his language
shifts to Bey, Tay, Chappelle, and his "Brat"
"Suss" pairs with my "Oh, man" and "Hey, Dude."
We're going to celebrate my 65 and a half in November
with rainbow candles, a gluten-free/vegan cake, and kisses.

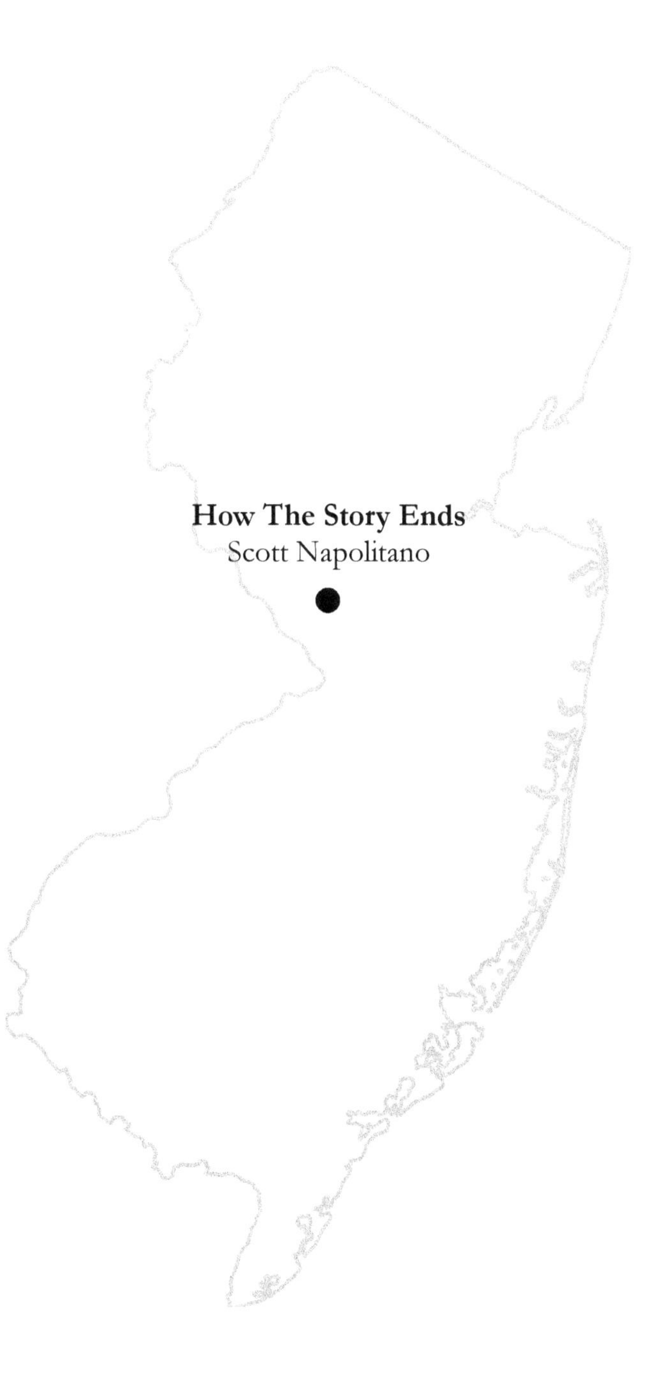
How The Story Ends
Scott Napolitano

This is how a drama begins.

The door at the end of the cement path is as average-looking as everything else in your neighborhood. Flower beds. A gnome standing guard. A sprinkler drifts steadily back and forth across the still-green grass – even Jersey's brutal summer sun couldn't kill its verdant hue. Despite the swelter, it's September, and school is starting up again. But I'm not in a classroom.

I'm here. Finally at the end of this story.

I approach the door slowly. I've been told this is a bad idea, but I can't help it. It's time – long past time, by nearly half a century.

I ring the doorbell and hear movement behind the door. The lacy blinds flutter as you check who's there. A delivery driver, perhaps? Someone selling solar panels or window replacements? No, just an average-looking middle-aged guy with tired blue eyes and a casual, non-threatening look, empty hands hooked through belt loops. The look is one I've practiced, and it puts people at ease: Nothing to see here, sir! Nothing in my pockets, nothing up my sleeve.

Detecting no cause for concern, you open the door.

Which is unfortunate for you since I am, in fact, armed. I'm in possession of six little words I've waited half my life to say, words whose grasp you believed you outran.

"I know the truth. It's over."

I teach film for a living, and if I was in one of those tense crime movies – something with Bogart or Cagney, maybe – this is the moment where your polite, confused smile would slowly melt away. Fear and anger would enter your eyes just in time for the sound of police sirens to fill the air.

But this isn't one of those movies. I don't see panic. Instead, you seem disconcertingly peaceful. Why?

Are you shielded by the fossilized arrogance gained from years of getting away with it? After all, on September 4th, 1977, you stepped out into the darkness blanketing Trenton State College and completely disappeared from history without a trace. No footprints, no bloody palm print on the wall or light switch, not a single hair left behind to confirm your identity. Gone.

Sigrid Stevenson had a future until she met you. She wrote about it excitedly in her journal. She felt like she had direction, perhaps for the first time in her adult life – just months away from finishing her Master's Degree. The city called to her, flashing chances to follow her passion for music into a teaching career, maybe even to find love – at least, as long as that love understood that her ambition came first.

You remember her, right? I bet you can still see her face when you close your eyes. Dark hair, blue eyes, a skinny frame dressed in clothes she often made herself. A little late to be a hippie or a bohemian, but still too early to be seen as truly independent. Her smile came easily once you made a connection with her. She was friendly – maybe too friendly, too trusting – and you sensed that quickly, don't you? Big Bad Wolf who hid his fangs behind the guise of someone she could trust, until...

I prayed for years that some new clue would finally, miraculously, be discovered. A deathbed confession, a memory jogged from a new article that pointed at a suspect. By intentional obfuscation or an unintended mistake, you slipped through the cracks long before I was born. No cross-examination, no picture in the paper with 'suspect' or 'person of interest' in bold letters under it. No day in court for the murderer who pulls off a vanishing act.

How often do you think back on that night in Kendall Hall? Do you feel a flicker of pride at what you got away with, or does your stomach turn at the mere thought of the horror you committed? After all this time, you must have at least considered what went on after you left. I bet you casually kept an eye on newspaper coverage until the unresolved story faded from memory. That was when you breathed a little easier, didn't you? Free and clear.

You wouldn't bury her body, but you did bury your past. Since September 4th, 1977, you put on a hell of a performance, worthy of a Lifetime Achievement Award at the Tonys. Method acting your way into the role of Joe Normal, Average Citizen on the Stage of Life. But after all these years, your show is finally over. All future performances cancelled.

You hadn't yet landed the part when you first stepped foot on the Kendall Hall Main Stage. That dark cave was for Previews, the place where you workshopped the Nice Guy persona. Or maybe you were angling to play the put-upon Patient Man, tolerating Sigrid's unauthorized squatting after the building had officially closed to the public for the night.

All she wanted was to be alone with the piano. But she wasn't alone that final night. You wouldn't let her be.

I back away as the cops read you your rights, the click of the cuffs over your wrists bitter music to my ears. Soon, detectives will ask you the question I've turned over for years in my head: What could she possibly have said or done that would make you beat such a peaceful girl to death?

We lock eyes as you're led to the squad car, but you'll never know how tired I am. How many sleepless nights I spent staying up reading old news articles about this story, my eyes burning from the strain of trying to pan for lost details in fuzzy photocopies no one has read since the Carter administration. Some details never quite fit, and it would keep me up even longer, wondering if this pursuit of justice was even possible.

You'll never know the time that I've lost to fix what you broke and what it took to get to this point. How it feels to be asked why bother? and then look in the mirror to wonder, is it still worth it?

Now I can state with confidence that, yes, it was all worth it. That's the dream, the happiest ending a story this grim can get.

That's how a fantasy ends. But the story within it, desperately waiting for someone to write its own ending, is true.

* * *

And this, this is how a mystery begins – with a question hanging in the air.

I've been asked it so many times before that one would guess I knew my answer by heart. Instead, I again slump in my rickety chair at the head of my classroom, still unsure.

"Why?"

For years, I've taught the mystery of Sigrid Stevenson's

death to my film students as an exercise in mystery film plotting. I was barely older than them when I first heard about The Ghost of Kendall Hall as a freshman at The College of New Jersey. That their teacher was young once, and also that he's long been involved in investigating a murder case, seems to blow their minds in equal measure. After all, what could the nerdy movie guy possibly offer the police aside from a deep-dive review of Zodiac or recommendations on the best camera angles to shoot a crime scene?

While seeking answers, we often wind up with a growing pile of questions. On a "spooky" freshmen campus tour in 2002, my classmates and I were told someone had been killed in the Communications building many years ago. One version of the story had her hung from the rafters by piano wire. Another had her pushed down the stairs. A jealous boyfriend had killed her for sure, the speaker insisted.

Always curious, I asked, "When was this?"

Blank stares, hemming and hawing. A startling lack of details – no victim name, no cause of death, hell, not even a general timeframe for when it happened. All we were told was that "a girl was killed in the building and it was never solved." I'd been a fan of mystery stories since childhood, and the discovery of this "urban legend" at my collegiate doorstep was tantalizingly enticing, if infuriatingly vague. My curiosity was piqued, and I began to dig.

Back in 2002, the internet wasn't the robust resource it's since become. Digital newspaper archives were hard to come by, and even if there were, that only would have helped if I had a date or a year or even a decade to start with.

In a stroke of luck, one of my professors remembered

the murder happened "over a break" in the late 70s. I can still hear the words that seem to hang over Sigrid's story like a storm cloud: "She wasn't supposed to be there."

When I finally found a crime retrospective piece dated to 1978, Sigrid's story received little more than a paragraph of coverage. But like a macabre game of MadLibs, I could finally start filling in those blanks.

Who was killed?

A 25-year-old graduate student, Sigrid Stevenson. Siggy to people she liked. Siggy to herself. A daughter and a sister. An aspiring teacher. An artist. A traveler. A young woman who liked to make her own clothes and pick fruit right off the tree as she walked and biked all over the area. Someone who 'would not suffer fools' according to those who knew her. Someone who 'trusted too easily,' according to many.

What was the crime?

She was found beaten to death on stage, nude, with her belongings nearby. Not a robbery. Not a break-in. Some papers first claimed she had been raped, though later reports pivoted to the official statement that she hadn't. Like so many official details from the initial investigation, important information seemed strangely drawn toward slipping through the cracks.

Where did it happen?

On the main stage of Kendall Hall at Trenton State College (now known as The College of New Jersey) in a locked theater. No signs of forced entry.

When was she found?

Campus Police Officer Tom Kokotajlo spotted her green Schwinn bicycle outside of the theater and called in the discovery at 11:29PM on September 4th, 1977. Labor Day festivities were still wrapping up, the new school year lay just ahead.

How was she killed?

There were indications that she'd been restrained at one point and the injuries suggest she had been bludgeoned without much of a fight. No weapon was ever found.

Why?

That goddamned question. The one that makes me grit my teeth with frustration because no answer will ever make sense, even from the lips of the demon who did it.

Every time I share the story, my students listen with shocked fascination and offer up their own questions. The more crumbs of information they get, the hungrier they are to ask for more. I know that feeling, so I share what I've learned. I tell them to think less like amateur detectives and more like writers and artists, to allow themselves to be free of mental constraints. These thought experiments strengthen their script plotting skills and they learn how to construct motivations, but it also strengthens their critical thinking skills. It doesn't take long for them to see the sheer power of an effective question. Some years, the students struggled to grasp very basic facts. Other years, their inquiries and interpretations made me approach the case from entirely new perspectives.

Whether their insights prove right or wrong, whether they see the whole picture or just a part of it, what's clear is that they connect with her. The mystery story plotting lesson and its subject stays with them. One year, an emotional senior said that they felt Sigrid sounded like one of them – a kindred creative who marched to the beat of her own drum.

Twenty years after I first heard the story and sixteen years after I first spoke with the police about the case, I was granted access to Sigrid's journal. I was drawn in by a passage in which she describes losing track of time and the world around her while she played piano. I get that. I'm sure all artists, no matter the medium, experience that kind of time travel. She loved that feeling, just as my students do. They empathize with this young woman who lived and died before their parents were born.

Storytelling is another kind of magic that allows us to time travel. It has the power to revive and sustain fragments of lost lives. In that way, every person with whom I share Sigrid's story becomes part of it – the magic of keeping her memory alive, and the burden of finding her story's ending.

After spending time getting to know Sigrid through her words and the events that unfolded around her, my students find their way to the same inevitable question: Why did this happen to her?

Sigrid could be quick to snap, becoming emotionally volatile when frustrated. She had, as one friend put it, "an acid tongue." Could she have burned a bridge or incited someone on their last nerve with an ill-timed remark?

Despite reports that she 'didn't have time for a boyfriend,' she certainly seemed to think she was sparking romantically with a few people over the years. Did she misinterpret a sign or inadvertently led someone on, sending mixed signals to a man who read it one way and reacted badly when she didn't follow through?

"How can this still be unsolved?"

The police in a sleepy town like Ewing weren't prepared for a crime like this – not on a holiday weekend, not ever. They followed leads that led nowhere, investigators looked at certain people more closely than others for reasons only they knew, and valuable time was burned through in the process.

I tell my students what one of the original reporters on the story once told me: the crime scene was handled so loosely back then that you would have guessed it was 1877, not 1977.

Sometimes those students look at me and ask the other dreaded question that evades an answer: Why do you keep looking into it?

There's no family bond or friendship connection linking me to Sigrid. No one made me swear an oath or assigned me the task of keeping the case in the public eye. There's no financial incentive, as it has even cost me money at times. Background checks, mileage, lost free time, dead end trips resulting in no new leads are the less-than-glamorous realities that true crime podcasts and TV documentaries tend to skip over.

For a while, I told people the answer they expected: I wanted to write a book or a screenplay based on all of this. That's an easy pill to swallow. This is a wild story. Scott's a writer. It makes enough sense to believe.

The real reason is far more complicated. I don't think I

can stop looking into the case. I don't think it will let me.

* * *

This is how a tragedy begins - with a seemingly innocuous choice.

Siggy, you think to yourself, you're going to return to campus.

You stare out the window of the Nassau Presbyterian Church in Princeton. It's quiet here, and you know you probably could stay longer, but you pine for the familiar sanctuary of the music building on campus.

For weeks, you've relied on the kindness of strangers to take you from Ewing to Princeton to New York, farther and farther north, out of the country, to the peak of Newfoundland. Hitchhiking during the Summer of Sam is a bold choice, one that some understandably call crazy. Despite the dangers you consciously or unwittingly ignore, you make it through New England into Canada unscathed.

You left the strangers who gave you rides with sketches you made along the way, exchanging phone numbers and addresses. You shared meals. In your journal, you documented all of the personalities you encountered like a naturalist observing wildlife. One trucker says, "You've got more nerve than Dick Tracy," like some kind of 1930s gangster. At a campsite filled with hitchhikers, you're happily given some beer and enjoy a campfire with fellow free spirits.

You love to travel. While still in the midst of your Canada-bound adventure, you're already daydreaming about thumbing your way out to Alaska once you secure your master's degree.

The world, in your eyes, is filled with beauty, and you keep your sketchbook close at hand to document simple, solitary moments out on the road.

Quiet moments alone don't bother you. You'll spend long stretches on your journey picking berries from bushes to quench your thirst and unroll your sleeping bag when the sun goes down, no motels needed.

This trip isn't your first time rebelling against expectations. It would have been so easy to stay in California where your parents hoped you'd continue your education, but the laid-back pace of the West Coast conflicted with your rigorous spirit. Visiting relatives in New York and New Jersey planted the seeds for crossing the country to attend Trenton State.

Your family has a history with money so you're not exactly coming from poverty, but you chafe against the notion of asking for financial assistance. You insist on paying your own way whenever possible, fixing guitars and helping clean up at the Jewish Community Center to put some money in your pocket.

"I wasn't brought up to ask for things," you once wrote, horrified at the mere idea of burdening someone. So you scrimp, you improvise, you sacrifice. English lessons for immigrants is something you do for free.

When looked at that way, your hitchhiking makes total sense. It's further proof of your desire to live independently. It may also hint at a naivete, or bravery, or a kind of unshakable optimism in man's good nature, or even a tendency we'd now match with a behavioral diagnosis. Or maybe you just liked to get away from everything. The world felt like a pretty dark place back in the 1970s. Why wouldn't you seek peace in gardening and walks in the woods and swimming in new rivers?

You'd just survived a rough semester! The end of grad classes was in sight, and soon, you'd be certified to teach! The future was approaching, and before it arrived, you needed to see the world and feel the sun and its renewal. You were jazzed at the idea of bringing on friends to play beside you at your final recital.

But an artist separated from their medium suffers until a reunion can be arranged, and your fingers ache for the piano after being away from the keys for so long. Once your adventures conclude, you'll make your way back to Mercer County as quickly as you can. You will never realize that, despite all the risks you took on your journey, the ultimate danger is at the end of the road.

* * *

All ghost stories need someone to haunt, whether literally or metaphorically. This next story is haunting – a trip through The Twilight Zone by way of suburban New Jersey.

It's October 9th, 1959. A bus full of Trenton State College students and staff are returning to campus after seeing Archibal Macleish's play J.B. on Broadway. The bus is struck by a gasoline truck, killing ten of its passengers. A memorial service is held on Kendall Hall's main stage, but you aren't there yet, Sigrid. You're seven years old and an entire continent away, safe and sound.

Now, jump to September 3rd, 1977. An off-campus

theater troupe puts on a production of J.B. in Kendall Hall's blackbox theater, and you attend its closing night show. It's the last known place where you speak with anyone. Almost 24 hours later, your body will be found a stone's throw from where you're watching the actors perform. One member of the cast, a self-proclaimed psychic, will give his thoughts on what happened to the police. Another person in the cast, acting as a police officer in the show, will become a person of interest decades later.

Cut to 2006, and I'm in Kendall Hall with another psychic who claims you aren't happy about what has happened to her story. She tells me you know I can help her.

No pressure.

I'm not a tin-hat wearing believer in all things paranormal; while I love reading Weird NJ Magazine as much as the next lore-loving nerd, I am of the 'optimistic skeptic' alignment.

The longer I've worked on this case, however, the more I notice the growing pile of inexplicable coincidences.

At a summer camp, I tell the story of the case to a couple of interested parties. My assistant walks over and tells me he knows all about this long-forgotten murder. He says his dad told him about it. As he turns his nametag around, I somehow sense who it will be moments before I can read the last name: Kokotajlo, the son of the man who found Sigrid. Small world, I guess.

When I was editing my student film inspired by the case alone in Kendall's basement, I was mere feet from the Green Room where you'd slept. When we filmed on the main stage, not knowing how close we were to where your body had actually been found, we put our actress in a blanketed pose that I wouldn't see repeated until I finally saw the crime scene photos a decade later.

I once had lunch with the director of J.B. was a man named Stanley Janusz. He was nice. Over appetizers, he told me he'd been a person of interest in the early days of the case. I tried not to flinch. He showed me props he'd kept from the show, including perfectly preserved plaster masks of God and Satan. I didn't share that my short film included a major character that, by pure coincidence, had his last name.

Your case seems to follow me everywhere. Every time I'd say "enough now," a new detail would arrive from strangers who had read newspaper articles about the film. Over time, an unlikely, unexpected community formed between people who had worked on the case, had known you as a classmate or as a neighbor, friends of mine who bounced around theories, and college students who heard your story and felt connected.

I once told my mother, "There's a part of me that wonders if this was what I was put here on Earth to do." She told me she hoped that wasn't the only thing.

Not long after state labs re-tested the DNA evidence on file, I suffered an aortic aneurysm. I needed emergency open-heart surgery to handle a genetic flaw in my heart that I never knew I had. Later, I was told that my survival odds had been somewhere south of one percent.

A friend who practices as a medium said, "You never were in danger. Sigrid was there the whole time with you the whole time. She wasn't letting you go anywhere."

Ghost stories, I've realized, are a gift and a curse. They are as much transparent echoes of our own lives as the spectral forms they purport are hiding in the shadows. Over time, a story loses its focus and the people who share it begin to paint over the facts with fictions and half-truths and 'I heard that..."'s which eventually overtake the true narrative. It is transmogrified, becoming something more dramatic and memorable at the expense of what made it real.

This is how a passionate, focused, complicated girl's life and death was reduced to a poorly-remembered cautionary tale told to scare teens when the night gets dark and the leaves begin to change. Over time, the tale becomes something new: a legend, factually fractured but remembered and retold.

True stories without endings may vanish, but legends have the power to endure.

Without the tale of The Ghost of Kendall Hall, I'd never have known about Sigrid Stevenson. My short film about her gained enough attention, it helped me get hired for my first teaching job. The biggest achievements of my adult life all have roots that can be traced back to asking questions on that ghost tour freshman year. I wouldn't be who I am today. It is a reality that hurts my heart and mind every time I think about it.

* * *

Even in my dreams, I can't seem to escape the story. As I drift off one night and 2025 fades away, a fantasy plays out.

I'm in front of a church in Princeton, and I know I have capital-m Magic somehow, the kind that only allows you to control it for a single shot, so you better use it wisely.

I appear silently in the back of the empty church and spot you at the piano, lost in the music. It's September 2nd, 1977, a day away from when you plan on sneaking into Kendall Hall. It's late, and you're undoubtedly hungry, probably in need of a shower. But these are secondary needs compared to the drive to return to what you were put on this Earth to do.

You revel in the acoustics of the space and the feel of the ivories as you let your true self be free. The song you're playing fills me with awe and dread, a classical piece brought to vibrant life.

When you finish the final notes, I clap. You look ready to scream, your blue eyes wide. But I shake my head and hold up a hand of cautious apology.

"I'm sorry," I say. "I didn't mean to scare you. I promise I'm not here to get you in trouble. I heard the noise and came inside." I hope you won't question how that's possible as you've never been caught here before. I know this because you write about it in the journal that will still be in police custody more than four decades later.

As you seem to recollect yourself, I can see you taking stock of me. I can only hope that the stories I've heard about you are true, that you'll show the overly-friendly side of your personality described by your classmates.

"I didn't even hear the door open. I thought it was locked," you reply, eyes wide. "I'm part of the church chorus and just got back from a trip up north and I wanted to make sure the piano was in tune," offering a half-truth with an embarrassed smile. "Maybe I wanted to make sure I was in tune, too."

"It sounded beautiful," I say. "Chopin?"

Your eyes light up. "Yes! Are you a fan?"

"Barcarolle in F-Sharp Major. Opus 60. I've heard that piece a lot…but never so lively," I say, swallowing hard to push down the emotions that engulf me. I only know this song because it's the last piece you were practicing before you died. Your sheet music was still at the piano, a teardrop of blood staining its corner.

"It's haunting."

You cock your head to the side, removing the bandanna from your hair that will very soon be found at the edge of the stage in a pool of blood. "Haunting?"

I run a hand through my hair. "Well…it has this feeling of an older time. Like I'm hearing something from a happy day in the past."

You smile. "That's why I like it!" you say brightly. "I love the thunder behind Bach or Beethoven, but this one…it just feels like sunlight." Then you frown. "It's tricky, though. I haven't practiced it in a while and I keep fumbling my fingerwork."

I sit in a pew a few rows down from you, giving you space, as though you're a deer that might bolt if I make too sudden a movement. Nodding to your backpack, sleeping bag, and discarded boots, I ask, "Are you planning on staying the night?"

Your back stiffens, so I wave the concerns away again and reply, "I won't say anything. I'm sure the priests here would want you to be safe rather than out on the streets."

Your shoulders relax. "Just the night. Tomorrow I'm headed back to Trenton State."

"Isn't the campus closed until classes start?" I say, playing dumb.

"Yes, but I know how to sneak into the music building and the theater," you say with a hint of pride. "My landlord won't be back for a few days and I can't get into the house. I'll hide out in the music building or the theater until then. The secretary of the music building gave me a ride to the supermarket so I have some food, and she told me no one is in that building until after the holiday."

This is the moment. I need to tell you to stay away and make you believe me.

I shake my head. "There's a play going on. I saw it. They'll be there all day and night. And on Sunday there will be cleanup to get the building ready for the start of classes."

You frown. There's no chance to practice if the building is going to be crawling with actors and crewhands. I can see you doing the math – where there's a play, there will also be campus police, and you've already had to deal with them in the past.

"Well, that ruins my plan," you say bitterly. "Now I don't know what to do."

Trying to be nonchalant, I slip a $50 bill from my wallet and place it on top of your sketchbook. You look at me with confusion and wariness. "For the music," I say simply. "That ought to be enough to rent a room for a couple of days here in town."

"That's…too generous! I can't accept this," you say, moving fast to hand the bill back to me.

I smile and back up toward the church's front doors, hands raised as if at gunpoint. "You shared your art with me, and artists deserve to be paid! You earned it. I've got money, but I've never heard Chopin played like that before. Thank you."

You shake your head, turning to put the bill in your purse. "No, thank you, Mr.--"

But when you turn, I'm already gone. I've done what I came here to do. That's all the Magic allows. Now I'll be the ghost you think about in the future rather than the other way around.

I open my eyes and it's the present day again. The church is empty. I depart and return to my car, but I can't shake the funny feeling that things seem off somehow. The car's mileage is different. When I return home, I find someone else's name on my mailbox. I check my phone and find that the app for my work email has disappeared.

A quick search online for 'Sigrid Stevenson murder' reveals no trace of an Unsolved Mystery episode, YouTube podcasts, or articles connected to your name or mine. A second search unravels your life story in short biographies for your work as a teacher and performer. A small exhibition at an art gallery in Princeton. A link to a performance in the 1980s at Carnegie Hall. Accolades from students at your retirement after a long career as a professor.

A photograph shows you far older than you ever got to be in life. Before the Magic, you were eternally 25, intensity and passion forever frozen in your eyes. But after, you are there on the screen with graying hair, wrinkles, a pair of thick glasses on your nose...but there remains the same gaze that screams just watch me fly.

You once wrote in your journal that you could face anything so long as the music stayed.

Your music lasted, and you were around to hear every note. I smile.

This is how the fantasy ends.

* * *

Magic isn't real. If it was, I'd be faced with the burden of choice. My entire adult life changed the moment I tried to understand your life. I've lived out years that were stolen from you.

Art and dreams are an escape from the horrors of reality. Your escape was found in music, and mine lives in stories. As I sit here listening to Chopin, time traveling through my writing, I know this is the only way we'll ever meet. With words, I create a world that lets us meet in the middle.

I remain steadfast in my hope that justice will someday be served. I still daydream about what I'll say to the unknown man when his game of hide and seek ends. Given the chance, I wonder what I would say to you.

I'm sorry.

Thank you.

You deserved better.

I'll keep telling your tale until things change. Until then… this is how the story ends.

Contributors

Adam Wilson

Cofounder of Read Furiously, Adam Wilson is an award-winning comic book writer and editor. His work includes *Last of the Pops*, *Brian & Bobbi*, *In the Fallout*, and *Helium*. He also edits the *Life in the Garden State* series with his partner and fellow Read Furiously cofounder S. Atzeni.

Find Adam Wilson online at:

lifeinasplashpage.com

instagram.com/amwilson81

Tetiana Horina

Based out of Kiev, Ukraine, Tetiana is an illustrator, and artist who specializes in sand animation.

Find Tetiana Horina online at:

behance.net/sandsmiles5d4b

instagram.com/tanya.go

Danielle Robertson

Danielle Robertson holds a BA in creative writing from SUNY Purchase and is a Tin House YA Workshop alum. Her short fiction has been published by Once Upon a Book Club, Terrorcore Publishing, and Haunted Words Press. She lives in northern New Jersey with her husband and their two children.

Find Danielle Robertson online:

daniellerobertson.net

danjvrobertson.substack.com

instagram.com/danjvrobertson

threads.com/danjvrobertson

bsky.app/profile/danjvrobertson.blsky.social

twitter.com/danjvrobertson

Elaina Battista-Parsons

Elaina is a writer and a teacher who wrote a short memoir (*Italian Bones in the Snow*) and a short story collection (*Heart and Salt*). She loves ice cream, antiques, dogs, and actively advocating for the LGBTQ+ community. Her newest memoir--*Chomp, Press, Pull*--is a full-on immersive experience.

Find Elaina Battista-Parsons online:

elainawrites.com

instagram.com/elainawrites

J. E. Krantz

Jason Earl Krantz writes epic fantasy and high fantasy novellas with scenery inspired by his own experience hiking through nature. To relax, he designs board games and creates video-game content for his few, loyal fans. He aims to reach the world with God's love and grace by sharing joy on common ground.

Find J. E. Krantz online:

jasonearlkrantz.wordpress.com

facebook.com/profile.php?id=61574459579053

Gaveth Pitterson

Gaveth Pitterson is a Certified Health/Wellness Coach, author, and radio host. With 20+ years in banking and 15+ in wellness, she's passionate about her faith, serving her community and helping others live healthy, fulfilling lives. She enjoys traveling, nature, and time with her family.

Find Gaveth Pitterson online:

gumroad.com/gavethpitterson
facebook.com/AuthorGavethPitterson
linktr.ee/CoachGavethPitterson

Midge Guerrera

Midge Guerrera, with her ever patient husband, Jack, spends half the year on a farm in Italy and the other half in a New Jersey high-rise. Her work has been published by Next Stage Press, Applause Theatre and Cinema Books, New Jersey Performing Arts Center Learning Guides, Anchorage Press, and the American Alliance for Theatre in Education. Her memoir *Cars, Castles, Cows, and Chaos* was published by Read Furiously in 2023.

Find Midge Guerrera online:

midgeguerrera.com

nonnasmulberrytree.com

instagram.com/expat49

facebook.com/midge.guerrera

A.J. Pellegrino

A.J. Pellegrino (She/They) has a B.A. in Creative Writing from Purchase College. She is the author of *The Path Home*, a standalone novella in Read Furiously's bestselling One 'N Done series. Their short fiction has been published by Read Furiously, Lavender Bones Magazine, and shortlisted by Spellbinder: A Quarterly Literary and Art Magazine.

Find A.J. Pellegrino online:

alycepellegrino.com

instagram.com/aprilsteahouse

bsky.app/profile/aprilsteahouse.bsky.social

aprilsteahouse.tumblr.com

tiktok.com/@aj.pellegrino

Patrick Lombardi

Patrick Lombardi is an author of humor collections *Junk Sale* and *Clear As Clay* as well as *The New Jersey Food Truck Cookbook*. A writer of both humor and horror, he is a lifelong New Jerseyan, where he lives with his wife and their son and turtle.

Find Patrick Lombardi online:

patricklombardi.com
patricklombardi.substack.com
facebook.com/patricklombardiwriter
instagram.com/patlombardi4/
threads.com/patlombardi4

Zoe Talbot

Zoe Talbot is an adjunct professor for the Writing Program at The College of New Jersey (TCNJ), where she earned her BA in English Secondary Education and MA in English Literature. When Zoe isn't engaging with literature, she's probably writing for Dungeons & Dragons or playing with her cats.

Find Zoe Talbot online:

instagram.com/quidpro.zo

Matt Lydon

Matt Lydon writes poetry, short stories, flash fiction, and yes, even scripts and draws sequential art stories. Matt is elated to be involved in another Read Furiously anthology. He'd also like to thank Liz, for always putting up with his silly goose antics. His books, *Worthing Through This*, and *Girls, They'll Never Take Us Alive*, are both published by Read Furiously.

Find Matt Lydon online at:

instagram.com/theemattlydonwrites
instagram.com/grocerystoredrummosheen

Itua Uduebo

Itua Uduebo was born in Lagos, Nigeria, graduated from Georgetown University with a degree in International Politics, and resides in New York, NY. He is currently working in the financial technology industry. His writing journey began in his college years and to date he has several essays, articles, freeform poems, and short stories published online and in print. His focuses are new adult fiction, urban literature, science fiction, thrillers, politics, racial justice, culture, and global affairs. His debut novel, *Parade of Streetlights*, was published by Read Furiously in 2023.

Find Itua Uduebo online at

ituauduebo.com

instagram.com/i.uduebo

tiktok.com/@ituauduebo

Danny Garrett

Danny is a truck driver and a harmonica player. He lives in Nashville, but wrote this story laying back in a sleeper cab at a New Jersey rest stop. You can follow his writing and music on Instagram @dannygarrettharmonica

Find Danny Garrett online:

dannygarrettharmonica.com

instagram.com/dannygarrettharmonica

Andy Chang

Andy Chang is an independent comic artist– based in New Jersey. He has made several children-friendly/all-age comics - such as *Add-Zero* and *Adventures of Sniffy* – prior to the creation of *Northwood Meadows*. Andy lives with his wife and three daughters, who all provides unlimited resource of inspiration and aspiration for *Northwood Meadows'* future comic art. His first two Northwood Meadows collections, *Lifestyle* and *Moments,* will be joined by *Sanctuary* in 2026 from Read Furiously.

Find Andy Chang online at

facebook.com/Chalkboardcomics

twitter.com/chalkboardcomics

Apara Mahal Sylvester

Apara is a published author and prolific writer. Her first book, a memoir titled *Angel Child*, was published in 2015. She has since written many children's books, several of which have cats as main characters. Apara resides in Somerset County NJ with her cats.

Find Apara Mahal Sylvester online at

aparamahalsylvester.com

Bill Hemmig

Bill Hemmig is the author of *Americana: Stories* and *Brethren Hollow*, both published by Read Furiously. His short stories appear in Read Furiously's *Life in the Garden State* anthologies, *The World Takes* and *Stay Salty*, and in the Toho Publishing anthology, *The Best Short Stories of Philadelphia, 2021*. He has had stories published in the journals *The Madison Review, Philadelphia Stories*, and *Children, Churches and Daddies (cc&d)*, and he is a three-time finalist in the New Millennium Writing Awards. Bill is also on the Board of Directors for the Arts & Cultural Council of Bucks County, where he has been a member of their Literary Arts Committee.

Find Bill Hemmig online at:

bucksarts.org/bill-hemmig

instagram.com /billhemmig

Alicia Cook

Alicia Cook, a writer from Newark, NJ, explores addiction, mental health, and grief in her work, including four award-winning poetry collections with Andrews McMeel Publishing. Sparked by her cousin's overdose, she advocates for families affected by addiction, delivers keynotes, and has appeared on PBS.

Find Alicia Cook online:

thealiciacook.com

thealiciacook.substack.com

instagram.com/thealiciacook

S. Atzeni

S. Atzeni is a multi-genre, award-winning writer and cofounder of Read Furiously with Adam Wilson. They are the coauthor of *The MOTHER Principle* graphic novel series, author of *The Legend of Dave Bradley* and the award-winning *W (h)ine and Cheese* in the One 'n Done series, and co-editor for Read Furiously's *Life in the Garden State* NJ award-winning anthology series. Sam Atzeni holds a B.A. in Professional Writing and Journalism and a Master of Arts in English from The College of New Jersey.

Find S Atzeni online at:

smatzeni.com

instagram.com/smatzeni

Margaret Montet

Margaret Montet is a college librarian and professor who writes and speaks about music, blending in elements of memoir, travel, art, and literature. She earned her MFA in Creative Writing from the Pan-European Program at Cedar Crest College, and a Master's in Music Theory from Temple University. In-between, she earned a Master of Library Science degree from Rutgers University. Her creative nonfiction has been published in *The Bangalore Review, Clever Magazine, Dragon Poet Review, Pink Pangea, Flying South*, and other fine periodicals and anthologies. Her collection of travel essays, *Nerd Traveler* was released in July 2021 by Read Furiously and her memoir *Brooklyn Family Album* was released in 2024. Her newest essay collection, *Music Lessons,* will be out in 2026.

Find Margaret Montet online:

margaretmontet.com

instagram.com/margaret_the_writer

Erinn Salge

Erinn Salge is a writer and educator located in northern New Jersey, but originally from Central New Jersey (it does exist).

Find Erinn Salge online at

instagram.com/erinnsalge

The Unforgiving Loop

A former graffiti artist based out of Central New Jersey, the Unforgiving Loop is now a father who retired the spray can and has since picked up the camera to document public art in all forms.

Find The Unforgiving Loop online:

instagram.com/theunforgivingloop

Kathy Kremins

Kathy Kremins is the queer daughter of Irish Catholic immigrants and a retired New Jersey public school teacher. She has two chapbooks of poems, Seamus & His Smalls (Two Key Customs, 2023) and Undressing the World (Finishing Line Press, 2022). Her full-length poetry collection is The Curve of Things (Cavankerry Press, 2024). Her first book with Read Furiously will be a part of the One 'n Done series. Called *Sipping a Cloud*, it is set for release in 2026.

Find Kathy Kremins online:

kathykremins.com

instagram.com/kreminsk

Scott Napolitano

Scott Napolitano, a born-and-bred Shore native, is a film teacher for Howell High School's Fine and Performing Arts Center program by day and freelance novelist/screenwriter by night. He was inducted into the Writers Guild of America at 25 and continues to develop projects for page and screen. Most recently he appeared in episode 4 (Murder, Center Stage) of Netflix's *Unsolved Mysteries*, discussing the life and death of Sigrid Stevenson. He lives in Central Jersey (yes, it exists) with his wife Jaime and four birds.

Find Scott Napolitano online at

scottnap.com

instagram.com/scottnap

bsky.app/profile/scottnap.bsky.social

A Note to our Furious Readers

From all of us at Read Furiously, we hope you enjoyed our latest title, *Disco Fries and Scenic Drives: Life in the Garden State.*

At Read Furiously, we wish to add an active voice to the world we all share by nurturing positive change in our local and global communities. It is with this in mind that we pledge to donate a portion of these book sales to causes that are special to Read Furiously. These causes are chosen with the intent to better the lives of others who are struggling to tell their own stories.

The causes we support encourage a sense of social responsibility associated with the act of reading. Each cause has been researched thoroughly, discussed openly, and voted upon carefully by Read Furiously editors.

To find out more about who, what, why, and where Read Furiously lends its support, please visit our website at readfuriously.com/charity

Happy reading and giving, Furious Readers!

Read Often, Read Well, Read Furiously!

Explore more New Jersey stories with the award-winning Life in the Garden State trilogy.

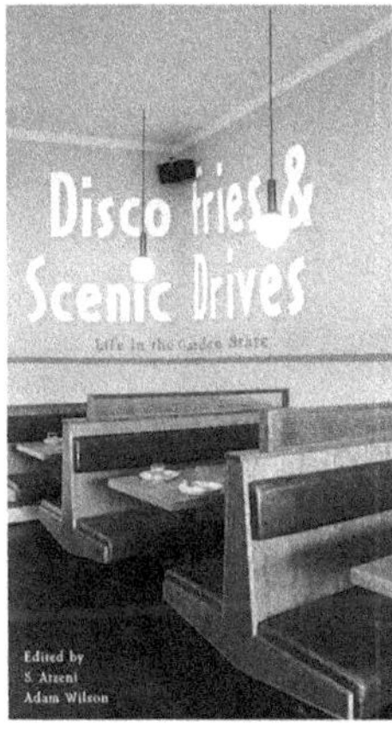

Available wherever books are sold. Learn more at
readfuriously.com/jersey